FANATICS

Special Agent Gus Novacek has orders from the President to stop Koji Shaguma's sinister Armageddon cult before it destroys the world. But it seems that Gus is always one step behind the murderous fanatics, as Armageddon strikes in Tokyo, Paris, London and finally New York. Then, a hijacked plane, bound for Algiers and rapidly losing fuel, is about to crash in the Atlantic with everyone on board . . . unless Gus can find a way to avert total disaster.

D0765986

STEVE HAYES
& DAVID WHITEHEAD

◆

FANATICS

Complete and Unabridged

LINFORD
Leicester

First published in Great Britain

First Linford Edition
published 2011

British Library CIP Data

Hayes, Steve.
   Fanatics.- -(Linford mystery library)
   1. Cults- -Fiction. 2. Terrorism- -Fiction.
   3. Suspense fiction. 4. Large type books.
   I. Title II. Whitehead, David, 1958 –
   823.9′2–dc22

ISBN 978–1–4448–0853–7

Published by
F. A. Thorpe (Publishing)
Anstey, Leicestershire

Set by Words & Graphics Ltd.
Anstey, Leicestershire
Printed and bound in Great Britain by
T. J. International Ltd., Padstow, Cornwall

This book is printed on acid-free paper

Part One

Paris

1

When Madeleine Chong left her rented house in the Parisian suburb of Les Lilas a little after ten o'clock that morning, she had no idea that her every move was being followed by a remote-controlled surveillance drone.

From a height of one thousand meters, the AIRROBOT AR100-B — a miniaturized video camera set within a thin circular frame that was powered by four small, helicopter-style rotors — could easily have been mistaken for an oddly-shaped bird, or perhaps something caught in the wind . . . if, that was, it was noticed at all.

Usually it wasn't.

Madeleine went down the steps to the sidewalk, took her crash helmet from the compartment under the seat of her scooter and stowed a Gucci shopping bag in its place. Then she pulled the helmet down over the sleek black hair she always

3

wore in a ponytail and fastened it under her small chin. When she was finally settled behind the handlebars of her Peugeot Viva-3 she headed west, toward Rue de Bellevue.

★ ★ ★

Elsewhere in the city, two men sat in the back of a parked Renault Megane painted in the distinctive red, white and blue livery of the French *Sūreté*, watching the clear but occasionally-wavering image being relayed back by the drone, which now showed Madeleine proceeding toward Place de la République.

One of the men, Inspector Henri Renard, glanced up from the small portable TV monitor and regarded his companion's sober profile. Renard was a small, elegant man of fifty. Gus Novacek, the big American beside him, was his complete opposite; tall, muscular, coiled, dressed untidily in a leather jacket, a T-shirt, old black jeans and lace-up Scarpa boots.

Renard said: 'Relax, my friend. She is

like a fly trapped in our web.'

Gus's lived-in face relaxed a little when he heard that. 'Did that line come out of the *Sûreté* manual, Henri?' he asked.

Renard chuckled. He had the mainland European's typically relaxed attitude toward life. The world might be coming to an end, but really, that was no excuse to hurry over your morning coffee and croissant. There was such a thing as taking life *too* seriously.

But it was different for Gus. Formerly a Special Agent with America's ATF — the Bureau of Alcohol, Tobacco, Firearms and Explosives — he had been selected for his present job by the President of the United States himself, and he took his responsibilities very seriously indeed.

In fact, he still remembered the day he'd got the call to fly from New York to Washington for the interview. A direct request from the President wasn't something you forgot in a hurry. Neither was meeting the President one-on-one in the Oval Office, shaking his hand, having him invite you to sit down as if you were old friends and then ask if you'd like anything to drink before you got down to business.

Gus had only shook his head, not trusting himself to say too much until he knew why he was here, and the President, reading as much in his expression, decided not to keep him waiting any longer.

'We live in, ah, 'interesting' times, Agent Novacek,' he'd said. 'A lot of things have changed since 9/11. We've come to realize just how fragile our liberty really is. You're familiar with the work of the National Threat Assessment Center, I suppose?'

'Reasonably so, sir.'

'Then you know that we as a country, and in a wider sense, we as part of the *world*, face a whole bunch of real and potential threats over the next ten to fifteen years — problems with South Africa, Jamaica, Trinidad, Pakistan, Algeria, Mali and others. We expect the world's terrorists to turn their attention from airlines to trains, buses and seaports. We have to accept that a number of rogue states will acquire a nuclear capability sooner rather than later. And the character of terrorism itself will change — heck, *is* changing. The focus is already shifting to various forms of illicit cyber activity — identity theft, the sabotage of computer systems all over the world, attempts to destabilize the world's financial institutions from within. Frightening, isn't it?'

'Yes, sir.'

'Well, don't let it worry you,' said the President. 'If my people do their jobs the way they should, those things need never concern the American public unduly. In any case, Gus — you don't mind if I call you Gus, do you?'

'No, sir.'

' — *you* will have other matters to concern you, if you decide to accept the job I'm offering.'

He looked at Gus for several long, thoughtful seconds. He saw a man in his early thirties, with a crop of short fair hair and dark brown eyes set in a tanned, rugged face. 'How many years have you worked in ATF — twelve?'

'About that.'

'Then you already have considerable experience with the particular threat I want you to deal with.'

'Sir?'

'Cults,' said the President softly.

As Gus frowned he went on: 'Now, I won't generalize over this. I realize that some of these organizations are largely harmless — sometimes even beneficial. The Mormons, the Jehovah's Witnesses . . . But others aren't quite so benign. We've all heard about Heaven's Gate and the People's Temple. The Twelve Tribes indulges in child labor. The activities of the International Churches of Christ — what used to be called the Boston Movement — are also highly questionable. The Black Muslims believe all whites are the Devil and as such should be wiped out. The Children of God specialize in manipulation and an extremely *ungodly* obsession with sex. The Unification Church spreads a message of destruction. And the list goes on. The Aryan Nations, the Christian Identity Church, the Ku Klux Klan . . .

'I believe some of these more extreme cults represent a threat that is every bit as serious as those posed by al-Qaeda, the Taliban, Hamas, the Armed Islamic

Group and others. And that is why I want *you* to head up SENTINEL.'

It sounded so much like something out of James Bond that Gus almost smiled. But one look at the President's bleak expression told him this was no joke.

'It's my own pet project,' he went on. 'You and your team — until I can push for more funding it's going to be small, I'm afraid — will monitor and assess every cult that fits the definition. You'll allow the harmless to practice their beliefs, as is the American way — but you'll also move heaven, hell and everything between to stop the militants and fanatics of these so-called 'doomsday cults' from damaging America and the world at large.'

Gus whistled softly. 'That's quite a task, Mr. President.'

'I understand that. But you won't have to do it alone. You'll liaise with any other domestic bureau or agency you need to, and I personally will make sure you receive every co-operation. But this goes wider than the United States, Gus. If you find evidence that these sicker elements mean to harm *us*, then you will have the authority to go anywhere in the world, to liaise with any opposite number or law enforcement agency, to find them and bring them to book.'

He turned and went to the window, where he looked out over the immaculate lawns. 'I don't expect you to make your decision right away,' he said. 'But I want you to know this. I didn't just pick your name out of a hat. You came highly recommended. You have a BA in Criminal Justice, so you're smart and literate. You can also handle yourself physically. And you're proficient in taekwondo, karate, savate and boxing, correct?'

'Yes, sir.'

'Then that gives you the brawn to go with the brains. You work with local, state and federal agencies on a regular basis. You've been trained in explosives and bomb-site investigation. You can handle everything from a Walther PPK to an AK-47. You know field ops, surveillance, arrest and undercover techniques. You're also a climber, aren't you?'

'Yes, sir.'

10

'What's given you greatest challenge so far?'

'Mount Vinson, sir.'

'Which is in . . . ?'

'Antarctica. Not especially high, but technically difficult.'

At last the President smiled. 'And there you have the final piece of the jigsaw,' he said. 'The quality that makes you the ideal candidate for the job, Agent Novacek. You *thrive* on challenge.'

Gus didn't answer right away. The President was offering him a massive responsibility and it would only be a brave or downright foolish man who took it on. But he didn't think the President had chosen him because he was a fool.

'I like the kind of challenge SENTI-NEL presents, sir,' he admitted at length.

'Then I believe we'll work well together, Gus,' said the President. And they shook on it.

★　★　★

And now here he was, eighteen months later, still hunting the world's fanatics

11

— in this case, a doomsday group known as Armageddon.

'Let's go,' he said.

Their police driver turned left out of Avenue de Friedland onto Place Charles de Gaulle, then left again to join the traffic along the broad, tree-lined Champs Élyseés. On the screen between Gus and Renard, Madeleine Chong crossed the Seine via the Pont de la Concorde and turned right at Quai d'Orsay.

'How long before she reaches the target?' asked Gus.

Renard shrugged as only a Frenchman can. 'Six, seven minutes.'

'It's gonna be tight.'

'I told you, my friend. Don't worry. Everything is in hand. You have the resources of every security agency in France at your disposal. Nothing can go wr — '

Just then the police driver braked hard.

As the car rocked to a halt, Gus looked ahead through the windshield and saw that they'd hit a mid-morning snarl-up. Traffic had reduced to a crawl.

He grabbed the back of the driver's

seat and urged: 'C'mon, *ami!* You've got a siren, haven't you? Use it, and get us the hell out of here!'

The police driver took his hands off the wheel and made a gesture of helplessness.

'You heard me!' Gus snapped, realizing he was running out of time. '*Recevez-nous autour d'eux!* C'mon!'

Exasperated, the driver unbuckled his seatbelt and leapt out of the car. Gus yelled incredulously: 'Where the hell's *he* going?'

Producing his whistle, the *gendarme* started gesturing to the drivers of the cars wedged ahead of him and yelling that they should move over to the curb. Being French, of course, the drivers totally ignored him.

Gus shook his head. 'I don't *believe* this.'

He looked down at the TV monitor again. Madeleine Chong was already turning left onto Quai Branly.

He thought: *She's almost there.*

Reaching a decision, he climbed over the seat and slid behind the wheel. Renard watched in surprise as he slammed the Megane into reverse and

13

rammed the vehicle backward into the car behind them. The wide-eyed driver there immediately vanished behind the white balloon of his airbag.

'*Mon Dieu*, Gus, what are you doing — ?'

'Not now, Henri!'

Gus shifted into first and then rammed the car ahead, pushing it forward several feet until it crunched into the car in front of it. He backed off then, wrenched the wheel sideways and floored the accelerator, bulldozing his way through the stalled and now-honking traffic until he reached the sidewalk.

'*Dieu me protège!*' cried Renard. '*Je suis dans les mains d'un maniaque!*'

Ignoring the outburst, Gus drove up onto the wide sidewalk and finally found the button that activated the two-tone siren. As it started blaring, pedestrians turned, saw him coming and jumped out of his way, then started shouting and shaking their fists in his wake.

'You *do* know,' yelled Renard, 'that what you're doing is strictly against the law?'

Chestnut trees sped past in a blur, as

did airline offices, car showrooms, brightly-lit shopping arcades and cafés. The needle touched 80 k.p.h. and Gus kept it there. The Place de la Concorde appeared up ahead, and the first chance he got he came down off the sidewalk, almost hitting a tree as he did so, and leaving a shower of leaves swirling behind him.

The lights ahead were green. That was something. He sped across the intersection and wrenched the wheel to the right. The Megane fishtailed into Place de la Concorde with a howl of tortured rubber and then they dropped into the Voie de Georges Pompidou.

Daylight was replaced by artificial amber light as he weaved in and out of traffic on the underpass. Then they were back out in daylight, briefly, before dropping into another length of tunnel.

Moments later the Megane roared back out into daylight, with the pillared front of the National Assembly building directly ahead of them, the Seine on their right, and a little farther along the Pont de la Concorde.

But the intersection ahead was now

blocked by cross-traffic coming off the Pont Alexandre III and heading onto the Avenue de Maréchal Gallieni to the left. Gus eased off the gas, then saw an opening and floored the pedal again.

The sleek blue-and-white bus came out of nowhere.

There was a crunching of metal and a loud shattering of glass. The bus crumpled the rear bumper and spun the Megane around in a sharp half-circle. Gus's airbag exploded, whacking him in the face. For a moment his whole world went black. Then, still groggy, he worked the seatbelt-release and shouldered the door open.

As he almost fell out into the street, he saw that the traffic had come to a complete standstill. The bus driver was staring at him through his windshield, pale-faced and — now that he knew he hadn't injured anyone — swearing. Pedestrians had stopped along both sides of the road to watch.

Renard staggered out of the back seat to join him, no longer looking quite so elegant. *'Idiot! Regardez maintenant que vous avez fait!'*

Ignoring him, Gus took one look at the way the bumper had been crushed in against the passenger's-side rear wheel and knew the Megane was finished.

He looked into the back of the car. The TV monitor showed Madeleine Chong just passing the Musée de Quai Branly.

Fists clenching, he looked around. Just before the collision a motorcyclist had been driving a few cars behind them. Now he parked his metallic blue Yamaha YZF-R1 by the curb and hurried over, taking off his crash helmet as he came.

'Je suis un docteur,' he called. 'Sont vous bien?'

Gus nodded. 'Nous sommes parfaits,' he replied, gesturing toward the bus. 'Mais vous feriez mieux de surveiller le conducteur d'autobus et ses passagers.'

As the doctor went by, intending to check on the bus driver and passengers, Gus flashed his SENTINEL ID and added: 'Excusez-moi, docteur. I'll take your helmet and keys, s'il vous plait.'

'Pardon?' asked the doctor, dumb-founded.

But there was no time to argue. Gus grabbed the helmet in one hand and plucked the motorbike keys free with the other, then sprinted for the Yamaha.

The doctor immediately started after him, yelling: *'Arrêt, voleur!'*

Gus jumped onto the bike, gunned the 998cc engine, and the machine leapt forward, the front wheel rearing up off the tarmac with the speed of his departure.

As he moved quickly to restrain the doctor, Renard shook his head in despair.

Ces Américains!

★ ★ ★

The road vanished beneath Gus in a gray blur. A bridge whisked overhead. Recklessly he continued to swerve in and out of traffic, only dimly hearing the angry blast of horns behind him.

Ahead was an intersection, where the traffic from the Voie de Berge Rive Gauche met that of the Quai d'Orsay. He turned right and joined it, and there, just peeking over the line of trees to his left he saw it, the tip of the tower.

The tip of the *target*.

The bike blurred on across Quai Branly and his destination grew more visible. He hung a hard left onto Avenue de Suffren, then left again onto Avenue Octave Gréard. In his ear-mike an undercover *GIGN* man said: 'This is *Sous-Lieutenant* Narcisse. I've got her in sight. Shall I move in?'

So there would be no mistake about it Gus replied in French: '*Non! Attendez-moi!*'

And then, finally, there it was — more than eighteen thousand individual pieces of steel held together by two and a half million rivets. Seven thousand tons of metal occupying a base area of two and a half acres.

Madeleine Chong's target.

The Eiffel Tower.

2

Madeleine Chong parked her scooter, took off her crash helmet and shook her head. A shiver ran through her glossy black hair. She swapped her crash helmet for the Gucci shopping bag in the compartment under the seat and took out a pair of distinctive white-framed wraparound sunglasses. When she put the glasses on, the day immediately turned sepia.

Squaring her small shoulders and holding her head high, the pretty twenty year-old Asian-American then blended with all the other tourists milling around within the tower's long shadow.

She was not the only fanatic there that day.

Elsewhere in the plaza, five other Armageddon cultists arrived by various means and promptly followed Madeleine's example.

Lydie Molyneux, a petite brunette of about twenty-five, chained her bicycle to a railing and calmly headed for the Tower.

Paige Cotton, a thirty year-old American, crossed the street and walked confidently into the throng of tourists.

Forty year-old Briton Derek Adams came down off the escalators at Bir-Hakeim Metro station and made the short walk to the Tower in less than two minutes.

Aldo Monte, thirty-five, closed the cab door behind him, paid the driver, then looked up at the tower and allowed himself a rare smile.

Tall and slim Erika Sandor, the penultimate member of the seven-strong cell, had long white-blonde hair and smooth, tanned skin. She was thirty, originally from Uppsala, in Sweden. She approached the Tower on foot, by way of the Parc du Champs de Mars.

Like Madeleine, all five wore distinctive, white-framed wraparound sunglasses and carried Gucci shopping bags.

★　★　★

Gus came to a less-than-careful skidding stop on Avenue Gustave Eiffel, scattering tourists before him. He was immediately confronted by Sub-Lieutenant Narcisse, the undercover *GIGN sous-officer*. Gus swung off the Yamaha and hooked the helmet over the handlebars.

'This way,' said Narcisse.

As Gus went after him, another taxi pulled up and a young, good-looking Indian man named Daksha Pawar climbed out. He paid the fare, then looked up at the needle-nosed steel landmark with a dreamy, faraway look in his dark hazel eyes. From this vantage it looked as if the Tower were trying to spear the blue sky beyond.

After a moment he reached into his jacket pocket, took out and donned a pair of white-framed wraparound sunglasses and then started forward.

He too was holding a Gucci shopping bag.

★   ★   ★

By now well on her way toward the yellow elevators that could be found in each leg of the Tower, Lydie Molyneux's attention was suddenly drawn by a commotion behind her. She turned and saw two men elbowing urgently through the protesting crowd. Recognizing one of them immediately, she was suddenly consumed by panic. He was no more than six meters from her, and coming closer all the time!

At last she had the presence of mind to turn away from him and the brawny, dark-haired man beside him, and whisper into the ear-mike hidden in the frame of her sunglasses: 'Shit! It's Novacek! Novacek's here!'

From elsewhere in the plaza, Derek Adams' voice came at her back almost at once. 'Lose him!'

Lydie was moving even before the order was given. She started pushing her own way through the crowd — and that's what brought her to Gus's attention.

He spotted the Gucci bag, the flash of white sunglasses against long, raven-black hair, pulled up sharp and said to Narcisse: 'There's another one! Grab her!'

Narcisse started wading through the throng, in pursuit.

Lydie kept moving, her catwalk figure accentuated by the tight jeans and exclusive red Skylon vest top she wore. She glanced back once, spotted the dark-haired man who had been with Novacek and quickly went from a fast walk to a jog. Narcisse followed suit.

Her nerve was slipping and she was ashamed of it. The Master had taught her better; that panic was just as powerful an enemy as Gus Novacek or the *Groupe d'Intervention de la Gendarmerie Nationale* or any one of the world's many other security agencies. But seeing Novacek here, the man who had hunted them so remorselessly now for more than a year, her nerve suddenly broke altogether. Heart racing, she reached into her bag, pulled out a .38-caliber Manurhin MR73 revolver and then turned, snap-aimed and fired.

Chaos exploded throughout the crowd. Screams and yells almost drowned out the sound of the shot as tourists threw themselves to the ground.

Narcisse, like all *GIGN* operatives trained to an extraordinary degree of readiness, reacted at once. He dropped to a crouch, ripped out a Sig Sauer P226 and returned fire. His single bullet punched through Lydie's sternum and dropped her where she stood.

She lay on her back, looking up at the electric-blue sky. To one side of her vision, the Eiffel Tower rose like a great black triangle pointing toward heaven. Into her ear-mike she whispered: 'I . . . I'm hit.'

A voice came back — Erika's, she thought. 'Badly?'

'Y-yes.'

Silence then, until a new voice spoke hypnotically into her ear, the deep yet serene voice of the Master.

'Come to paradise, my child,' he said.

Lydie nodded just as Narcisse approached her, gun still in hand. She reached into her shopping bag and closed her fingers around a small, airtight container attached to a digital timer. Her finger clicked down on the timer and the device started counting down from 5.

Narcisse quickly wrenched the bag away from her, tore it open, looked inside, saw the time tick down from *3 . . . 2 . . . 1 . . . 0* —

Then the bomb went off with a blinding flare and a dull, racketing thump of sound, and he was thrown backwards even as the explosion released its deadly payload in the form of a seemingly innocuous, heavier-than-air cloud of white vapor. Within seconds everyone around them was choking, coughing, screaming for help and clawing at their streaming eyes.

Narcisse, who suffered the greatest exposure, died within minutes. The gas — chlorine — caused a rapid build-up of fluid in his lungs. Cause of death: pulmonary edema.

In essence, he drowned on dry land.

★   ★   ★

Moments before the shots were exchanged and the bomb went off, Gus spotted Madeleine Chong walking unerringly toward the elevators. He broke into a run, still elbowing tourists aside. Hearing the slap of his boots against the ground, Madeleine turned an instant before he smashed into her. They both crashed to the ground, her sunglasses went flying and she snarled at him, her face suddenly that of a spiteful cat.

He punched her on the jaw. Her eyes rolled up into her head and she went limp.

As more *GIGN* operatives came out of nowhere, Gus tore the Gucci bag from the girl's grip, opened it, saw the device inside, the digital timer ticking down from 8 to 7 to 6 to 5 —

He took it out. It looked so much like a bomb that everyone around them recognized it at once and immediately started to flee. One of the *CIGN* men said: 'Do you want me to — ?'

'I got it,' said Gus, and he quickly pulled the red and green wires loose, effectively disarming it.

That was when they heard the two gunshots, followed moments later by Lydie Molyneux's bomb going off.

Gus jumped up and thrust the Gucci bag to the nearest *GIGN* man. 'Bomb squad! *Now!*'

As the *GIGN* man started speaking

into his ear-mike, Gus again checked out his surroundings. Somewhere along the line their intelligence had been flawed. They'd been led to believe that the girl, Chong, was the only cult member targeting the Tower today. Now they knew better —

He spotted Daksha Pawar at once, because he was the only other person in the vicinity who was still heading for the Tower. He was also holding a distinctive Gucci shopping bag and wearing white wraparound sunglasses.

'Keep looking for others!' Gus barked, then sprinted after him.

But Daksha had already made it to the nearest elevator. Gus saw the outer-cage door closing even as he drew closer and knew he was never going to get there in time to stop it.

Instead he changed direction and headed for the stairs.

It was a bad move.

Having heard the gunshots, explosion and the general sounds of alarm surrounding the arrest of Madeleine Chong and the disarming of her bomb, tourists were now starting to flow down the stairs in panic. Gus struggled against the tide, but doubted if he'd be in time to intercept the elevator on the first level.

As the elevator continued to rise almost sideways, following the inward curving angle of the tower's leg, the people inside began to look uneasy. Something was going on around the tower base and whatever it was it sounded ominous. Through the large elevator windows and beyond the passing network of girders they could see *CIGN* men in gasmasks standing around Lydie Molyneux's corpse, men from the Civil Defense Bomb Squad containing some sort of device in what appeared to be a large metal bin, another woman, her black hair worn in a ponytail, being escorted to a waiting police car. Only Daksha remained calm, staring straight ahead through his shades, a small, happy smile tilting his mouth.

At last the elevator reached the first level. Everyone but Daksha decided to get off, go back to the ground level and leave the area until they could find out what was going on. Daksha waited calmly for the doors to finally close again.

They closed just as Gus, panting now, reached the first level, and as the elevator itself climbed at its vertigo-inducing sideways angle out of reach he flung himself at the outer cage doors, tore them open and then threw himself into the shaft. He caught one of the cables dangling from the elevator's underside and swung wildly back and forth as the cable yanked him up toward the second level.

A few moments later the upward rush slowed, then stopped. The elevator doors opened. Daksha got off and walked directly toward the Jules Verne Restaurant, his Gucci bag held loosely in one hand.

As the doors slid shut again, Gus swung himself back and forth like a human pendulum until he was able to reach out and grab one of the girders enclosing the elevator shaft. He held on tight, then let go of the cable and grabbed the girder with his other hand. He climbed hurriedly, using the network of girders like a ladder. As the elevator shot away from him, he reached the outer cage gates and was just in time to see Daksha vanish into the restaurant.

Damn!

Inside the restaurant, customers, bus-boys and the Maitre d' were crowded against the windows, all looking out to see what was going on in the plaza below. Ignoring them, Daksha headed for an unoccupied table, sat in one of the orange-backed chairs and reached casually into his bag.

One click of a button and it was done: the countdown was underway.

10 . . . 9 . . .

He placed the shopping bag under the table so that it was hidden by the hanging tablecloth, then rose and joined the crowd at the windows.

Gus entered the restaurant at a run. He looked around. Daksha was nowhere to be seen. Then he turned his attention to the people gathered around the windows and spotted him almost at once. He drew his matt black FN-Five-seven semi-automatic and crossed the room with a determined stride.

'Hold it!'

. . . 8 . . . 7 . . .

31

All heads turned, Daksha's included. His expression was chillingly empty. He didn't even seem to think about what he did next, he just did it. He grabbed the nearest woman and yanked her in front of him so that she became a human shield. As he did so he produced a pistol of his own, a Glock, and pushed the short barrel hard against her temple. Only then did he seem to really come to life.

'Drop the gun or I kill her!' he shouted in broken English.

Gus's lips tightened, but he wasn't giving his gun up for anything. To prove it he snap-aimed at a nearby table, where an elaborate swan carved out of ice was surrounded by a display of mouth-watering desserts. Not missing a beat, he popped one cap and the swan exploded in a silver spray.

'I'll put the next one right up your nose,' he warned.

Daksha, mad-eyed now, retreated quickly, dragging the woman along with him. The other patrons used the opportunity to dive for cover.

Still Gus advanced.

. . . 6 . . . 5 . . .

Gendarmes poured into the restaurant behind him. Without looking around Gus waved them back. 'Don't shoot!' he yelled in French. And then, to Daksha, in English: 'Give it up.'

For just a moment he looked as if that was exactly what the young Indian wanted to do. But in the next second he whirled around and fired a shot at the nearest window. It burst outward, shards of glass winking in the now late-morning sunlight. As patrons started yelling or screaming again, he thrust the woman away from him, threw himself up onto the frame and quickly climbed outside.

Gus turned toward the *gendarmes.* 'Look for the bomb!'

He dropped onto his stomach and scoured the floor between a forest of chair- and table-legs. He saw the Gucci bag under a table on the far side of the room.

He leapt up and ran toward it, scooped it up, looked inside.

. . . 4 . . . 3 . . .

Fuck!

He yelled, 'Get out of the way!' and ran back the way he'd come, toward the window Daksha had shattered.

. . . 2 . . . 1 . . .

He threw the bag through the jagged hole as everyone around him took cover. The bag flew out into the air and then —

It blew with enough force to rock the restaurant, but the cloud of deadly white gas that erupted with it was quickly shredded by the stiff wind, and Gus knew from previous experience that it would dissipate and become all but harmless before it floated to earth.

He came up out of his crouch, ignoring the spontaneous, relieved applause generated by his actions. He hopped up onto the window, crawled outside, looked up. Daksha was already thirty feet above him, climbing the girders with reckless speed, the howling wind pulling at his long black hair. Gus took a deep breath and started up after him.

He hadn't gone far when Daksha looked behind him. He couldn't believe anyone would be dumb enough to come after him and in panic sent a couple of hurried shots back at his pursuer. Gus pressed himself flat to the cold girders, wincing as the bullets screamed off the steel. A moment of near-silence followed, and then Gus snapped his head skyward again. Daksha had resumed climbing.

Gus quickly followed, picking his way higher, his climber's eyes automatically seeking out and finding the best foot- and hand-holds. Above him Daksha was slower, clumsier, and fighting a losing battle with his nerves.

Then Gus heard a buzzing sound behind him and, holding tight, looked over one shoulder. A sleek Eurocopter AS350 *Ecureuil*, decked out in the blue and white-striped livery of the *Gendarmerie*, was edging in closer so that the police marksman in the open doorway could get a bead on Daksha.

Gus took his right hand off the girder and waved the chopper away. As he did so he got a dizzying view of Paris stretched out far, far below him.

Then there came another bark of

sound: Daksha had also stopped and fired twice, once at the departing helicopter, once more at Gus. In that moment it seemed to Gus that their eyes met and locked, Daksha's through his sunglasses, though the distance between them was still too great for Gus to be sure. There was a moment, though, a connection between them. Then Daksha snarled and tossed his empty gun at him and resumed climbing.

He couldn't hope to get away. Other *gendarmes* were already waiting to intercept him on the observation platform at the top of the Tower. He stopped climbing when he saw them, looked back down at Gus, and beyond him he saw the sprawl of the city, the sculpted parks and paths around them, the shadow of the tower itself tumbling across the olive-green curve of the Seine.

Gus closed the distance a little more, yelled: 'There's nowhere to go! Give it up!'

Again Daksha was a picture of uncertainty — until the same soft, hypnotic voice that had invited Lydie to

36

paradise whispered through his ear-mike.

'Come to me, my son. Paradise awaits.'

It all became so *clear* then.

Daksha turned himself around so that he was facing outward. Gus felt something unpleasant stir in his belly, a feeling of dread and inevitability, something he knew was going to happen and which he was powerless to stop.

He thought, *Shit*, and he yelled: 'No! Don't — '

Daksha dove off the tower as if he were diving into a swimming pool. He dropped so gracefully that he seemed to be flying, and not falling at all.

He flew past Gus in a blur and Gus couldn't help but keep watching his descent until Daksha finally hit one of the outward-curving legs of the Tower and smashed against its iron girders.

There was a collective gasp from the crowd surrounding the monument as the body parts of Daksha Pawar that didn't get stuck in the network of steel spattered over them.

★ ★ ★

Having regrouped below, Derek Adams and Erika Sandor shared the collective horror at what they'd just witnessed. Aldo Monte watched with complete detachment, while Paige Cotton grinned with grudging admiration.

'Don't you just love that kind of dedication?' he said.

Derek and Erika gave him a strange look, as if they were only now really seeing him for the first time. Aldo was content simply to raise one very dark eyebrow.

'I think we had better get out of here now,' he said.

3

Madeleine Chong sat at the table in the middle of an otherwise featureless interrogation room. She had been staring directly into the two-way mirror on the opposite wall for the past thirty minutes, and though he would never admit it, it was starting to freak Henri Renard out.

But then, he reasoned, that's what she was hoping to do. These people, it was all about mind games with them. Still . . . in handcuffs and orange jail fatigues she should have looked beaten, the loser in today's little game. She didn't. And that was freaking him out a little, too.

He continued to watch her through the mirror as Gus finally entered the room and sat across from her. Madeleine pointedly ignored him.

'Having fun?' he asked at last.

She made no reply.

'How would you like to get out of here?' He kept his voice low, almost confidential, but Renard, watching from the darkened room next door, heard every word.

At last Madeleine looked at Gus. On the surface at least she was young and attractive. But a closer look into her eyes showed a bitterness and cruelty that vandalized anything else that might otherwise have been appealing about her.

'And who the fuck are you?' she demanded.

'The guy who can make it happen,' Gus replied in his soft, coaxing tone.

He dug out his wallet, opened it and showed her his ID. It told her who he was and the kind of clout he could wield, but she refused to be impressed.

'So you're a cop,' she shrugged. 'Big deal.'

'Big enough to get you *out*.'

When she made no reply, he leaned closer and said quietly: 'All you have to do is tell me where Shaguma is.'

The hate-filled eyes glared at him. 'Get fucked,' she said.

He only smiled. He wanted her to think that this wasn't personal, it was just

40

business. 'Okay, I'll make it easier for you. Where's his next hit?'

'You'll find out soon enough, asshole. And I promise you, thousands are going to die.'

'More innocent people?'

'The people Armageddon targets are not innocent,' she said, speaking the mantra automatically and without inflection. 'They're all part of the capitalist, corporate-minded society that's destroying the earth.'

'Commuters on the Tokyo subway?' he asked, arching one brow. 'Those kids in the Berlin school? What kind of bullshit has Shaguma *fed* you, Madeleine?'

'The truth,' she said doggedly.

'You want the truth?' he countered. 'Okay. *Here's* the truth. You're what, twenty years old? Jesus Christ, you've still got your entire life ahead of you. Do you *really* want to spend it in a six-by-nine cage?' He gave her a moment to think about that, then: 'I'm offering you a *deal*, Madeleine.'

'You're offering me shit,' she sneered. 'The Master has given me eternal life.

Beat *that*, asshole.'

Gus looked at her some more, as if he were trying to figure out just what kind of creature she really was, but she refused to look away, and there was unholy pride in her for what she'd tried to do this day. Without another word, he left the room.

In the office next door, Renard said: 'We'll keep hammering at her. Never fear. She will break down eventually.'

Gus raised his eyebrows. 'Guess you must've been at lunch when that other guy, Pawar, took an air-walk off the Eiffel Tower.' He felt his frustration rising again and wondered why people like Henri still couldn't get it through their heads that this wasn't just another bunch of cranks they were dealing with. 'She's not bullshitting, Henri. These jerkoffs really believe Shaguma's *God*.'

'They're brainwashed. Programmed.'

'Of course they are. But how does it happen in the first place? How do ordinary, right-thinking, *normal* people get sucked into stuff like this to begin with?' It was a question that had plagued him ever since he'd taken up the job, a question for which he had yet to find a satisfactory answer. 'What is it about Shaguma, anyway? The guy's nothing but a charlatan. Anyone with half a brain-cell should be able to see that.'

But they didn't. They wanted too badly to feel special, as if they'd been somehow *chosen*. And Shaguma was too plausible, too charismatic.

Information on Koji Shaguma's past was sparse at best, but SENTINEL had managed to discover a few things about him. The only son of an impoverished couple who made straw mats for a living, he'd been born in 1964 or 5, in a nameless little village along the banks of the Japan's Ooi River. He'd received minimal education but had quickly developed delusions of grandeur and ambitions above his station. In late adolescence he'd started dabbling in politics, and when that hadn't worked out he'd gone to live in Nagoya, where he'd opened an acupuncture clinic, then a yoga school, and started selling fake remedies that guaranteed to cure everything from flat feet to bowel cancer.

He was a con man, pure and simple. And yet the tourists he'd deliberately targeted, the people who were so hungry for his particular brand of mysticism and flummery, happily ended up giving him every cent, penny, euro and rupee they possessed to make sure they secured their place in the paradise he promised.

As his wealth and power increased, and his *Harumagedon* cult spread from country to country, he had finally come to Gus's attention. Shaguma preached that Armageddon was the only true path to paradise, that only by wiping out the 'unbelievers' could the *true* believers enter heaven.

They'd started their program of 'cleansing' in Tokyo, detonating chlorine gas bombs on the subways and killing more than fifty people in the process. Then they'd bombed two Catholic schools in Berlin, killing more than a hundred children. They came out of nowhere, committed their acts of terror and then, in intelligence-speak, went dark again, until the next time. And there hadn't been a single thing Gus could do to stop them, until today.

'Of course they're programmed,' he said again. 'But that doesn't make them any less dangerous, Henri. If anything, it makes them the most dangerous enemy of all, because they have nothing to lose and everything to gain. Obey Shaguma's will, follow Shaguma's orders to the letter, and you guarantee yourself the ultimate reward — a place in heaven. It's like the Chong girl said just now. Who the hell can beat *that?*'

Part Two

London

4

The Cumberland Hall Infirmary on Maiden Street was opened in 1960. Six years later the London Board of Guardians designated it as a children's hospital. In 1972, by which time it was in private ownership, it began to specialize in the care of physically and mentally challenged children. By 2010 business was booming.

And yet when Paige Cotton arrived and paid off the taxi, he looked up at the faceless building and wondered if he'd ever seen a more depressing place. All that was missing was a sign over the door quoting Dante's *All hope abandon, ye who enter here.*

He heard the screaming long before he reached Elkin Ward, and stopped just inside the doorway. The ward was untidy, with a hastily-mopped tile floor, sickly nicotine-yellow walls and grimy windows. Beyond the glass he saw the Houses of Parliament and the London Eye as if through cataracts.

The long, high-ceilinged room was lined with narrow beds — old, ugly NHS stock from the seventies with rust-flecked frames. Each bed was occupied by a child who stared blankly at the ceiling, or screamed and thrashed, or was strapped down. There was no visual or aural stimulation that he could see, nothing that even came *close* to treatment of any kind.

But then, the Cumberland Hall Infirmary wasn't really *about* treatment. It was simply a discreet holding-pen for the mentally and physically damaged, a place where those who could afford it could brush their less than perfect offspring under the metaphorical carpet. There was no future here for these children. They'd been abandoned as much by the staff as by their families; the staff, who were conspicuous on this dreary Monday morning, largely by their absence.

As a sociopath, Cotton had always happily combined his abnormal lack of empathy with abnormally immoral conduct. But today even he felt a momentary stab of shame, and for a moment was tempted to turn around and leave again. But then he glanced down at the Hamley's shopping bag in his right hand and almost before he realized it he was walking between the two rows of beds, searching for the boy he had come to visit.

He found him in the last bed on the left, in a pitiful state of neglect. He was six years old and his name was Alex. He was sitting up in a tangle of stained sheets, staring into space, absolutely motionless. He wore a dirty hospital gown and he smelled of soiled diapers. He deserved so much better than this.

Cotton wrinkled his nose at the stink but leaned forward and kissed the boy's head gently, then stroked his matted hair.

The boy was totally unaware of his presence.

At last Cotton reached into the Hamley's bag and brought out a teddy bear he had just bought in Regent Street. He tried to make the boy take it in his tiny hands, but the fingers were unresponsive. The teddy bear tumbled onto its side next to him.

The rattle of trolley wheels suddenly intruded upon Cotton's dark thoughts. He turned as a nurse entered the ward and started preparing medication for the children. He could guess what kind of medication it was — Ritalin, Zoloft, Paxil or Prozac. Something to knock the kids out and let the staff get on with the really important business of reading magazines and surfing the internet and flirting with each other.

Cotton stroked the boy's hair one last time and then walked back down the aisle toward the nurse.

'Excuse me . . . ' he said softly.

'Just a minute,' she replied without looking up. She was young, with short red hair, and was so thin she looked brittle.

Cotton grabbed her with his left hand and brought his right, the one holding the switchblade, up to her angular face. He popped the blade: it flicked out of the handle like the tongue of a poisonous snake. The nurse stared at it, blue eyes wide, lashes flickering.

Holding the tip of the blade to the

nurse's throat, Cotton said: 'You see that little boy over there? Alex?'

She nodded, but he doubted that she actually knew him by name.

'That's my son,' he said. 'I'm leaving now. And if he isn't cleaned up by the time I come back, I'm gonna cut your fuckin' throat. You got that?'

Too scared to speak, the nurse could only manage another shaky nod.

Cotton let her go and walked out.

★ ★ ★

Koji Shaguma sat in the library of the mansion he had bought — under an assumed name, of course — in the heart of the Berkshire countryside.

'You have disappointed God,' he said in a soft, deceptively gentle voice as his heavy-lidded, almond eyes glided from Derek Adams to Aldo Monte, from Monte to Erika Sandor. 'He anointed me and it is my responsibility to bring Armageddon to the governments of the world. But you have failed God . . . and you have failed me. You allowed the

French to stop you from gassing those people.'

Derek studied him from beneath shame-lowered brows. Shaguma was many things, but above all he was an enigma. He sat in a high-backed chair to one side of the massive fireplace, swathed in white robes, tall by Japanese standards, trim when Derek had first joined the cult but now starting to thicken at the waist. He was in his forties, Derek thought. Few if any knew for sure. He wore his black hair long and tangled, center-parted so that the bangs framed an oval face with skin deliberately bleached to a lighter shade of its natural hue. Faint tracings of brow formed a ridge above his eyes, a flattened, Nubian nose dropped to almost feminine, heart-shaped lips. His moustache was ragged and wispy, as was the short, straggly beard at his chin.

'It wasn't so much the French, Your Holiness,' Derek said at last. 'It was the American.'

'Novacek,' Shaguma said quietly.

When he made no further comment, Derek said: 'Do you still want us to go ahead with the London gassing?'

'Of course. But God has told me to make a change to the plan.'

'A change?' asked Erika.

Shaguma reached for the bell-pull hanging beside the fireplace and a moment later a girl who looked no older than fourteen — one of the Master's many concubines — came in carrying a tray of juice drinks. When she had served everyone and left again, Shaguma said: 'To our success in London.'

They drank.

'Master,' said Derek, 'what's this *change* you mentioned?'

Shaguma gave him a benevolent smile. 'God is replacing you,' he said.

Derek frowned, not quite sure he understood.

A moment later he understood perfectly.

His face suddenly twisted into a grimace of agony, his body hunched in on itself, he convulsed, his teeth clenched and he toppled forward, out of his chair. He twitched briefly, the nails of his fingers scratching frantically at the carpet.

Foamy saliva trickled from his lips. Then his eyes went wide and rolled up into his skull and with startling abruptness all movement within him ceased.

He was dead.

Enjoying the shock he saw in Erika's tanned face, Shaguma said: 'Aldo, you will be in charge in London — and God trusts there will be no more mistakes.'

Aldo opened and closed his mouth for a moment, more surprised than horrified by what he'd just witnessed. 'No,' he said finally. 'No. No more mistakes.'

They were about to move on to other business, Aldo and Erika pointedly ignoring the body on the floor as if it would be a breach of etiquette to acknowledge it further, when there was a knock at the door and Cotton entered. As soon as he saw the corpse he smiled coolly.

'Another dedicated follower, Master?'

Shaguma overlooked the insolence in his tone, and also allowed the half-hearted bow that followed it to pass unchecked. 'What is it you want, my son?'

'A hundred thousand dollars,' Cotton said.

Shaguma showed no surprise. His expression remained one of empty serenity. 'Why do you need this money?'

'Personal reasons.'

'Here, we have no personal reasons. We are all one.'

'I know — but I still need the money.'

Shaguma frowned at him and said reasonably: 'If I gave money to every one of my children who believed they needed it, we couldn't continue our work.'

Cotton glanced around the room, which spoke of almost incalculable wealth — the accumulated and ongoing donations from Shaguma's legions worldwide that gave and gave and then gave some more to keep in his favor.

'You *do* understand, don't you?' said Shaguma. There was a subtle challenge in the way he said it, as if he wanted to provoke Cotton into doing or saying something rash that would give him the excuse he needed to deal with him once and for all.

But all Cotton said was: 'Perfectly.'

Deciding to bide his time, he bowed politely and then left the room.

As soon as the door closed behind him, Shaguma turned his gaze back to Aldo. 'After he completes all the trigger mechanisms,' he said gently, 'send him to paradise.'

5

When she was about thirty nautical miles out of Heathrow Airport, Captain Renee Forester throttled back to 350 knots and slowly descended to around 2000 feet. Beyond the Concorde's distinctive moveable nose-cone (locked down now, in anticipation of the landing), the wispy clouds parted to reveal the patchwork quilt of rural Buckinghamshire and, in the middle distance, the urban sprawl of Middlesex. She spotted Wembley Stadium, the King George VI and Staines Reservoirs, the constant flow of traffic along the M4, the lazy blue snake of the River Thames curving east toward Essex.

'Reducing speed for the approach,' she said. 'Call the tower on frequency one-one-nine-point-seven-two-five.'

Her co-pilot, Mark Turner, did as instructed, his movements as precise and confident as hers. 'Good afternoon, Heathrow, this is Speedbird Concorde

Five. Do you read me? Over.'

'*This is Heathrow, Speedbird Concorde Five. Reduce minimum speed for approach. The wind is southerly, with zero six.*'

'Zero six, roger that.'

'Landing gear down,' said Renee, her green eyes moving busily from one set of dials and switches to the next. 'Standby final checklist.'

'Standing by,' said the navigator.

'Passing 4 DME . . . now.'

She turned off the GPS and manually lined the plane up with the nominated runway. Her digital speedometer dropped to 250 knots and the plane descended another thousand feet. By the time she was twenty nautical miles out, the plane was descending at 190 knots.

'One-seventy . . . one-sixty . . . one-fifty . . .'

She made a near-perfect textbook landing, which was only to be expected from someone of Renee's experience, and then taxied toward Terminal 3.

The flight from New York had taken a little under three hours, but it wasn't over just yet. As today's passengers left the plane Renee and Mark went through the after-landing check. Controls, locked. Landing lights, off. Anti-Collision strobe lights, red. Ignition, normal. After-landing check, complete.

'I suppose Gus'll be waiting for you?' asked Mark, grinning.

'I don't know. I hope so. But the last time I saw him on CNN, he was playing Tarzan on the Eiffel Tower, so I'm not holding my breath.'

When she finally reached the passenger gate, flight bag in hand, Renee looked around, expecting to see Gus' battered face at any moment. She was disappointed when she found no one waiting for her. But then, their relationship had never been easy. When she was in London he was in New York. When she was in New York he was in Berlin, or Paris. Few relationships could survive under those circumstances, and yet theirs did for the simple reason that, when they were together, the time they shared was nothing short of magical.

Mark and the cabin crew emerged from

the arrival tunnel behind her. Seeing her all alone, Mark asked if she'd like a lift home to her small flat in Chelsea.

She shook her head. 'No, thanks. Hopefully he'll be along in a while.'

'Well, if you're sure. See you Monday.'

She waited another ten minutes, and when it became obvious that Gus wasn't going to make it, she decided to make her own way home.

'Captain Forester?'

She turned at the unfamiliar voice and found a tall, underfed man in a gray chauffeur's uniform staring at her. He had a sober face and a stiff-backed, squared-shoulder bearing that spoke of military service.

'Yes?'

'My name's Mountgrave, mum. I have instructions to take you directly to the Savoy.'

'Do you, indeed?'

'Yes, mum,' he replied almost mournfully. 'Strict instructions from Mr. Novacek.'

He led her outside to a silver Rolls-Royce. He opened the door for her. She climbed inside and soon they were

62

purring along the M4, heading toward central London and The Strand. She arrived in style forty minutes later and received another message, this one from the clerk behind the desk.

'Good afternoon, Captain Forester. Here's your key. I'll have a boy carry your bag up to the River View Deluxe.'

She raised her fine eyebrows, impressed. 'The River View Deluxe?'

'Yes, Captain. In the meantime, Mr. Novacek said he'll join you as soon as possible.'

The suite proved to be every bit as grand as it sounded. The long, stylish living room was comfortably furnished and the view was breathtaking. An unopened bottle of champagne — Dom Perignon 1996 — sat in an ice bucket on the table, beside two fluted glasses, a bouquet of deep red roses and a card. Renee kicked off her shoes and read the card. It said: *Have I told you lately that I love you?* And when she opened it the message concluded with: *I do, you know.*

The no-nonsense captain in her immediately thought: *Creep.* But the woman inside her melted a little at the sentiment, and all at once the need to see him was stronger than ever.

She checked out the bedroom — it contained an almost impossibly large bed — and then stripped off and took a long, hot shower in the marbled bathroom. Water spilled down over her eyelids, across her high cheekbones and dripped from her strong jaw and diamond chin.

Now thirty-seven, she'd started flying when she was sixteen and taken her first solo flight on her seventeenth birthday. Flying was the only thing she'd ever really wanted to do, and after her middle-class parents had realized just how serious she was about making a career out of it they'd sent her to America, where training was faster and cheaper.

Four years later she'd returned home to Ashford in Kent with her Commercial Pilot's and Airline Transport Pilot's Licenses. A job as First Officer with British Airways had followed. She'd been lucky: the aviation industry had been expanding rapidly at the time, and because the mandatory retirement age for pilots back then had been sixty (it was now sixty-five), there had been plenty of opportunities for newcomers. As a pilot she'd started her career on 737s at Gatwick. After that anything else was a stroll in the park.

Many of her colleagues were surprised when she decided to leave BA and go to work for Speedbird, but she'd never seen it as a bad career move. Although the Concorde SST had been retired in 2003, it was still the fastest commercial aircraft ever built, and as such one she had always harbored a desire to fly. Now she did just that, regularly crossing the Atlantic in record time for businessmen, celebrities and aficionados of the iconic aircraft who still got a kick out of flying at supersonic speed.

At last she finished showering and switched off the water. She was tall and toned, with natural red hair — plastered down now — usually worn with a left-hand part, long on top and short at the sides.

When she stepped out of the shower she saw him leaning against the bathroom doorway, grinning at her.

'How long have you been ogling me?'

'Nowhere *near* long enough.'

'Well, show's over, Novacek,' she said, and dropping her towel walked straight into his arms.

'I'm sorry I couldn't meet you from the airport,' he said after they kissed. 'I got hung up.'

'On the Eiffel Tower?'

'Cute.'

She sensed the frustration in him and said: 'The Armageddon business again?'

He nodded. 'Always the Armageddon business,' he sighed. 'But I'm here now, and we're gonna make every moment count.'

He went into the living room and as she slipped into a robe she heard him pop the champagne cork. When she joined him, he was pouring champagne into two glasses.

'Champagne?' she said. 'Roses? A card professing undying love, and a suite that must have cost two arms and both legs? Okay, I give in — what have you done with the *real* Gus Novacek?'

He handed her one of the glasses. 'This *is* the real Gus Novacek. Or rather, the new, improved model. The one who's decided he's hopelessly in love with Speedbird's loveliest pilot — '

'Is it *me* we're talking about here, or Mark Turner?'

He tilted his glass toward her, suddenly serious. 'Do you know how much I really love you?'

'A whole *bunch*, I hope.'

'A lot more than that.' They clinked glasses, sipped their champagne, then settled together on the sofa. As she snuggled against him he said: 'How was your flight?'

'Better than your day in Paris.'

'*Anybody's* day was better than my day in Paris.'

'At least you stopped that Shaguma character from gassing those people.'

'I guess. But I'm no nearer to stopping Shaguma himself.'

'Well, I'm sure the French are thrilled. They'll probably give you a medal and a kiss — '

She'd been about to drink more

champagne when she realized there was something in the bottom of her glass.

It was a diamond engagement ring.

'Oh, Gus,' she said, fishing it out. 'It's *beautiful.*'

'Will you marry me, Kitten?'

She put her arms around his neck and kissed him hard.

'Is that a yes?' he said.

'A very *definite* yes,' she replied. 'But why?'

'Apart from all the obvious reasons, you mean?'

'I mean, why *now?*'

He made an awkward gesture. 'The truth?'

'Always the truth.'

'Well, there are all these great tax breaks we can take advantage of — '

She punched him, hard enough to make him wince.

'Okay, okay,' he said. 'I also happen to love you.'

'You've loved me for a long time.'

'That's true.'

'Then, why propose *now?*'

He hesitated.

She knew his problem instantly. 'You're

down again, aren't you? Because of Shaguma.'

He knew it was pointless to deny it. She'd always been able to read him so easily. 'I'll get over it,' he said. 'I always do. But sometimes . . . sometimes it's like you can only take so much of man's inhumanity to man. Then you either give up, or replace all that bad stuff with something good. Something that's *better* than good.'

'And you think getting married would help with all the bad stuff, is that it?'

'The bad stuff's only part of it,' he said. 'A tiny part. I don't want to marry you because I need a quick fix. I want to marry you because I love you, and I want us to be together, to have fun together, grow *old* together.'

She studied his face carefully, then said softly: 'What happened up there? On the Tower?'

His expression changed and he quickly downed some more champagne. 'A man died,' he replied. 'One of Shaguma's acolytes, a young Indian guy. He tried to gas a bunch of people he didn't even know and then, when he realized he couldn't get away, he just took a dive right off — '

Unable to finish the sentence, he changed it to something else instead. 'That could have been me, Ren. Not doing it deliberately, but because of some stupid mistake, a missed handhold, a slip. They could have been mopping *me* up off that plaza.'

'Don't say that.'

'But it's true. And when I realized that, I realized something else as well. That I want to savor every moment I have with you. That I want to *marry* you.'

She looked at him a moment longer, feeling a sudden welling of emotion but knowing that tears wouldn't solve anything. She swallowed and said: 'Have you seen the size of the bed in this place?'

'Not yet.'

She forced a smile. 'Well, put that glass down and step right this way . . . '

★ ★ ★

Later, in the afterglow of sex, Renee said: 'Gus, this was the most romantic proposal I could've wished for.'

He grinned. 'It *was* pretty neat, wasn't it?'

She snuggled closer to him. 'Let's spend the whole of tomorrow right here, in bed.'

'You're reading my mind.'

'It'll all work out just fine,' she promised. 'You'll nail Shaguma eventually. And then we'll celebrate with a quiet little wedding . . . buy a house in the country and live happily ever after, just you, me and little Gus Junior.'

She was only half-joking, but as soon as she said it she felt him tense.

'Honey . . . ' he began.

She stroked his cheek gently. 'It's all right. I know the subject of babies makes you uncomfortable. But really, Gus, it'll be fine. I promise.'

'Why can't it just be us?'

She raised up onto one elbow. 'Gus, we've been over this a hundred times. I love you very much. I want to marry you. But I'm four years older than you, and my biological clock's ticking away. I want a baby. *Your* baby.'

'Why would you want to bring a child into *this* shitty world?'

'Maybe because I *don't* think it's so shitty.'

'It is, believe me. I've *seen* it.'

'You've only seen *part* of it. What about the rest? All the good things you risk your life to protect?'

He felt his dark mood returning. 'But we're always on the road,' he argued without much conviction. 'Most of the time, the kid wouldn't even *have* parents.'

'That's a lame excuse, and you know it. I'd give up flying in a minute.'

'You'd better not. You make too much money. We couldn't live on my salary alone.'

'Oh, come on — '

'All right, it's not just the money. But . . . this job would be hard enough with just you to worry about. With a kid as well . . . '

His voice trailed off. He didn't really have the words to say what the extra responsibility would mean. He felt that it would make it almost impossible for him to do his job, and even though she knew that as well as he did, she looked at his profile in the darkness and then slowly, deliberately removed the engagement ring and handed it to him.

He took it, too startled to do otherwise. 'Hey, wait a minute . . . ' he began.

'I'm sorry, Gus. Maybe we'd better forget about the marriage thing until we're both sure what we really want from it.'

'But . . . you can't say *no*.'

She looked at him for a long, unnerving moment longer. Then she said: 'Gus — I just *did*.'

★　★　★

The chauffeur, Mountgrave, collected them in the Rolls early the following morning. That told him something. The frosty silence between Gus and Renee, as he drove them to Renee's flat in Chelsea, confirmed it.

After Renee got out and disappeared into the block of flats without a backward glance, he looked at Gus in his rear-view mirror and said: 'I'm sorry your weekend didn't turn out as you expected, Mr. Novacek.'

'Me, too.'

'Perhaps a little pick-me-up, sir? I know a nice little pub just off Kensington High Street . . . '

'No. Drop me off at St. Paul's, will you?'

Mountgrave nodded wisely. 'Ah, yes sir. A chat with the Maker. That helps sometimes, too.'

But that wasn't quite what Gus had in mind.

6

Overnight, Park Lane and parts of Oxford Street and Marble Arch had been cordoned off, and regular traffic diverted to other routes. A little after dawn the crowds began to arrive, and by the time the new morning really got underway they were pressing heavily against the temporary barriers set up along each thoroughfare. But still people kept coming, men, women and children of practically every age and nationality, and soon mounted policemen had to herd the overspill into nearby Hyde Park, where the latecomers could watch the motorcade on the massive TV screens that had been erected there for the purpose.

The mood of the crowd was amiable and expectant. It seemed to the authorities that everyone wanted to catch a glimpse of Joseph Kimani, the man of the moment. And Kimani, the new Secretary-General of the United Nations, whose heartfelt messages of peace, tolerance and hope had caught the imagination of the masses, did not intend to disappoint them.

A little after ten-thirty, a tall Goth dressed in a flowing black overcoat and black jeans pushed his way through the crowd, an old-school boom-box — a throwback to the 1990s that was mercifully silent at the moment — balanced on one shoulder. He had jet black hair and pale skin, and had used subtle shades of gunmetal-gray eye shadow to accentuate his eye sockets and cheekbones. His lips were painted black.

Spotting him trying to scale one of the temporary barriers, a policeman in a fluorescent yellow high visibility jacket hurried over and snapped: 'Oi, you! Stay back!'

The Goth pointed toward the Underground station on the other side of the street. 'I gotta catch a train,' he said in an American accent.

'Sorry, mate, you'll just have to wait till the Secretary-General's been and gone.'

The Goth shrugged, nodded and raised

his free hand to show that all was cool. Beneath the wig and make-up, Paige Cotton knew better than to argue the point and risk getting arrested for disturbing the peace. He *did* have to get to Marble Arch Underground station, but he still had plenty of time, provided the Secretary-General didn't keep them all waiting too long.

Ten minutes later he sensed a reaction in the crowd and looked right, to where Joseph Kimani's motorcade was finally coming into sight.

A Metropolitan Police motorcycle escort came first, then a black car full of security agents, and then Cotton spotted the elegant, white-haired African black man standing tall and lean in the back of a convertible stretch-limousine, waving to the crowd. He was in his early sixties, and had about him an air of patience and serenity that made him appear almost saintly. But those who knew him, and were familiar with the wry twinkle that could so often enter his gold-flecked eyes, knew Kimani was neither saint nor sinner, just a man of high principles and great compassion.

The motorcade drew closer. Kimani waved and smiled, smiled and waved. Television cameras mounted atop broadcast vans captured every moment. The crowds yelled and cheered, waved back and hoisted banners that said *The UK Welcomes Kimani* or *Kimani — We ♥ You*. Cotton knew that these scenes would be repeated over and over again as Kimani continued his much-publicized world tour.

And then, as he watched, he suddenly saw the smile leave the Secretary-General's face. Next Kimani leaned forward and down in order to speak to his driver. A moment later the motorcade drew to a halt and to everyone's surprise, Kimani opened his door and climbed out of the limo, looking immaculate in his charcoal-gray Jay Kos suit. To Cotton's alarm, the Secretary-General started walking directly toward him.

Cotton watched him approach. He didn't understand why Kimani had singled him out and didn't like it, either. In the next moment, however, he saw his mistake. Kimani hadn't been attracted by *him;* he'd spotted a little girl in a wheelchair nearby, who had been holding a small bouquet of flowers out toward the passing motorcade.

Kimani strode toward the little girl, his expression showing how touched he was by her gesture. Around him, his security guards formed a protective ring, their eyes everywhere at once.

Kimani took the flowers, nodded to the girl's mother and then bent down to plant a tender kiss on the girl's head. The crowd went wild. Cotton seized his moment, scaled the barrier, dodged quickly across the street and then hopped across the barrier on the far side. He elbowed through the crowd there and went down into the Underground station.

As he came off the escalator and onto the eastbound Central Line platform, he saw that there had been some sort of delay, and the platform was more crowded than usual for the time of day. Cotton wandered down toward its far end. Here a dark-skinned businessman was standing aside from the other travelers, and carrying a briefcase in his left hand. He looked smart but ordinary, just another commuter trying to get from A to B. The only odd thing about him was his white-framed wraparound sunglasses.

He saw Cotton through their sepia lenses and tilted his head in a small, near-invisible nod of acknowledgement. Cotton nodded back. This was Raul Iara, a follower originally from Santa Luzia, in Brazil.

Cotton wandered back the way he'd come. The subway tunnel smelled warm and stuffy. At the other end of the platform he made contact with Wayne Mason, a tall, broad-shouldered man in jeans, T-shirt and muddy boots, who was holding a lunchbox in his left hand. He appeared to be some kind of manual worker — hardly unusual when one considered the amount of construction going on in central London right then. The only odd thing about him was his wraparound sun —

'*Keira!*'

The echoing cry had such urgency in it that everyone looked around, Cotton included. The speaker was a young woman Cotton had noticed in passing on his way up toward Mason. She had a cute-looking blonde kid with her, who'd been tossing a little red ball in her hands. He saw at once that the child had dropped the ball and it had bounced toward the edge of the platform and the child, Keira, had gone after it, heedless of the risk.

Cotton reacted without thinking about it. He performed a nimble sidestep and trapped the ball underfoot before it could roll off the edge of the platform and onto the live rails. He then picked it up and smiled at the girl, who looked up at him uncertainly, a little scared by his wild appearance.

'Here you go, princess,' he said.

He gave her the ball and received a shy smile in return.

'You be careful next time. Don't get too close to the edge, otherwise you might fall.'

The girl turned and hurried back to her mother, who gave Cotton a smile and mouthed *Thank you*. She was surprisingly attractive, he thought.

It was almost a shame she had to die.

* * *

The Rolls dropped Gus outside St Paul's Cathedral and then rejoined the flow of traffic heading for Blackfriars Lane and the Old Bailey. Gus looked up at the massive building for a moment, his eyes tracing the pillared front, the spire-topped clock-tower that marked its westernmost tip, the curve of its dome against the leaden sky, and then headed for the neat little gardens at the rear.

Here, he took off his jacket, tied it around his waist, studied the nearest wall for a second or two — and then started climbing.

* * *

The Eastbound Central Line train thundered through the tunnel from Lancaster Gate to Marble Arch. Because of the earlier delay, there was standing room only, and even that was at a premium. In

the first swaying carriage Erika Sandor
had gradually allowed the other passengers to force her back down the aisle
toward the pale gray door that led to the
driver's compartment, which was where
she wanted to be. She was dressed in a
business suit, held a briefcase, and wore
white wraparound shades.

Just before the train entered the station,
she set the briefcase down behind her so
that it was propped against the driver's
door. She made the act appear so casual
that few people even noticed it.

Then the train was rushing into the
station and slowing, and several commuters started elbowing toward the automatic
doors, Erika among them. She stepped
off the train without a backward glance
and more people immediately tried to
squeeze inside. No one realized that she
had left the briefcase behind.

She joined the flow of travelers heading
for the escalators, her expression showing
emotion only once, when she saw Cotton,
who immediately fell into step behind
her.

The boom-box he had carried into the

station now sat where he had left it beneath a red two-seater bench.

Raul and Mason also headed for the escalators. But Raul no longer carried his briefcase, which he'd left propped against a disused information booth. Mason was no longer in possession of his lunchbox, either. That had been dropped covertly into a rubbish bin.

The little girl, Keira, and her mother boarded the train. Keira threw-and-caught her little red ball a little faster, because train journeys were always more exciting than going places in Daddy's car.

* * *

When it arrived at Lancaster Gate less than thirty seconds later, the next eastbound Central Line train was slightly less crowded than its predecessor, which was now taking on more passengers just under a mile ahead, at Marble Arch. As it came to a stop and the doors shushed open, a black man wearing a gray *Transport for London* uniform and white wraparound glasses tapped on the driver's

84

window and mouthed: *Let me in*. The driver had never seen him before, but that didn't mean much. Drivers worked different shifts, drove different trains on different lines. With more than three thousand on the books, you couldn't be expected to know everyone.

He unlocked the door, and as the other man stepped inside he asked: 'What's the problem?'

Saleman Tubec, a twenty-five year-old cultist originally from Mogadishu, Somalia, said: 'No problem.'

Then he stabbed the driver with a long, thin-bladed knife. The blade went up under his ribs, punctured his pericardium, and killed him instantly.

Tubec lowered him to the floor of the cab and then grinned as he prepared to take over the controls.

★　★　★

The motorcade had gone, and the crowd was slowly dispersing. Cotton and Erika emerged from Marble Arch Underground station and lost themselves in the throng.

85

Raul and Mason came next. They passed a priest who had been watching the motorcade with an expression of great enjoyment. He wore wraparound glasses, identical to theirs.

He was Aldo Monte.

As they walked off, he took a small remote-control device from his pocket. To the casual observer it might have been a cell phone. He looked at it a moment. Perhaps he was reading a text. Then he pressed a button on the device, replaced it in his pocket and walked unhurriedly away.

Far below ground, on the eastbound line platform, the CD tray on Cotton's abandoned boom-box suddenly slid open. An ominous white vapor began to belch from inside it.

The clasp on the briefcase Raul had left behind him suddenly snapped open. Gas fumes began to pour out.

The lid on Mason's lunchbox, left in one of the bins, popped up. It too began to release toxic chlorine gas.

Unaware of the problem, the driver closed the automatic doors and prepared to pull out of the station. The briefcase Erika had left propped against the driver's door clicked open, filling the cab and the first carriage with poison.

Everything was going according to plan.

* * *

The commuter who had been sitting closest to Erika's briefcase suddenly cleared his throat, then cleared it again. He flicked his head a little, reached for his collar, ran a finger around it, as if to loosen it. No good — he still couldn't breathe.

A moment later he fell forward off the seat and went into cardiac arrest.

In the driver's cab it was a similar story. The driver began to cough, there was a burning sensation in his eyes and throat, his eyes started to stream and then he bent forward and threw up.

On the platform, the travelers who'd been unable to cram themselves aboard the train were suddenly seized by a collective fit of coughing. At first no one thought anything of it. But then, as the struggle to clear airways became not just difficult but practically impossible, people started to panic.

Those who could began to stagger toward the escalators. Those who were more seriously affected by muscle weakness, spasms and dizziness stumbled and fell, and those behind them stumbled and fell also.

A woman at the end of the platform lurched forward, clutching her throat, bumped blindly into the end of the stalled train and then fell off the platform onto the live third rail. There was a snap of sound, a flash of near-white light. The body jerked and fell loosely into the gulley beneath the rails, still quivering.

Inside the train, startled passengers started stabbing fingers at the door release, which had been disabled by the driver before he was taken ill. Panic spread quickly. People started hammering at the windows. Others began to push toward the manual interconnecting doors at the end of each carriage, not realizing that they were already as good as dead.

By now the first carriage looked more like a slaughter-house. Keira's mother beat frantically against the windows, trying to break the toughened safety glass and allow fresh air into the passenger car, but it was impossible. Her blows quickly grew weaker, and she died thirty seconds after her daughter.

★   ★   ★

Lancaster Gate fell behind them and Saleman Tubec watched the tunnel ahead rush toward and then past him. Central Line trains rarely went above 20 m.p.h. The stations were so close together that there was never any point. But now Tubec pushed the throttle all the way forward and the train responded immediately, quickly picking up to thirty, forty, fifty —

An oval of light appeared in the darkness ahead, partially blocked by the train that was stalled in the station beyond. It rapidly grew larger, larger —

Tubec's train smashed into the back of the one in front and crumpled like an accordian. The force of the impact rammed the first train forward with a wrenching, brake-locked scream of iron against steel and finally pushed it off the tracks. Passenger cars battered each other and then jack-knifed, gouging great, jagged chunks out of the curved station roof. Couplings snapped, glass shattered, debris was hurled everywhere and the entire station was filled with the squealing crunch of metal against metal, metal against stone, metal pulverizing flesh.

Saleman Tubec saw none of his handiwork. The passenger cars behind him quickly compressed together and he died almost instantly. Then this mangled wreck derailed too, the off-kilter cars wedging themselves in the tunnel and slicing through the thick electrical cables that ran along the tunnel walls.

The entire network died a sudden, terrifying death.

7

The area around St Paul's Cathedral had almost come to a standstill. After the first person had glanced up, seen Gus perched on the façade just below the dome and then stopped dead, thinking he was about to commit suicide, others had quickly followed suit until the narrow pavements were now bottlenecked with onlookers.

Traffic had slowed, too, as drivers noticed the crowds with their pointing fingers and craned necks, and then leaned forward over steering wheels to see for themselves what they were looking at.

If Gus was aware of his audience, it didn't show. He gazed off across the city, his moody thoughts dominated by Renee and how he'd lost her, maybe for good.

He had no idea how long he'd been sitting there when his cell phone buzzed. He took it out. The caller ID told him it was Chief Superintendent Nick Williams of SO15, the Metropolitan Police's

Counter-Terrorism Command, and his prime contact with New Scotland Yard.

Something unpleasant chilled Gus' spine. 'Novacek,' he said grimly.

'It's Armageddon, Gus,' said Williams, his tone tighter than usual. 'They've gassed the Underground at Marble Arch.'

'How bad?'

'As bad as it can get, if the preliminary reports can be believed. Where are you?'

'St. Paul's. Pick me up.'

He looked down at Cannon Street, almost three hundred feet below. Then he started his descent.

★ ★ ★

By the time they reached Hyde Park, the entire area had been sealed off. For a mile in every direction the city had been evacuated: driving that final distance in Nick's silver BMW 5 was like driving through London after the end of the world — empty, abandoned, wholly unnatural.

Then they saw the urgent bustle of life ahead — a seemingly chaotic crush of police cars, fire engines, ambulances and railway incident support units parked everywhere around the station, light-bars flashing, and on the other side of the yellow police tape a jumble of BBC and ITN, CNN and SKY TV news vans.

'Jesus Christ . . . ' Williams whispered under his breath. He was a short, hard-muscled man in his early forties with cropped black hair and direct hazel eyes. 'They weren't kidding when they said it was major.'

Large portable ventilators had already been set up to suck the dust and poisonous gas out of the wrecked station. Emergency service personnel were dashing in every direction, some in bright yellow, some in bright orange. Bulky figures in HAZMAT suits were carrying body-bags out of the station to a long line of waiting black vans.

Gus felt sick.

Williams' driver braked and as they climbed out they were met by an ashen-faced man Williams introduced as Chief Inspector Jimmy Cox. Jimmy, he said, was based at West End Central, the police station nearest to the disaster, and as such had been first on the scene. 'What's it like down there?' Williams asked him.

'A fucking nightmare,' Cox replied, adding hurriedly, 'if you'll pardon my French. We've estimated the number of dead at approximately eight hundred to a thousand.'

'*Christ*. Survivors?'

'We're still searching. There'll be some, I think, but not many.'

'Go on.'

'Well, practically the entire network's gone down — that's about five hundred trains, two hundred and fifty stations. We've got passengers trapped in tunnels anywhere between one and two hundred feet below ground, we've got them stranded on bridges sixty feet high, and stuck in tunnels below the Thames. Like I said, sir: It's a fucking nightmare.'

Williams indicated the station entrance. 'Has it been made safe down there yet?'

'We've been shoring it up as we go.'

'Come on, then.'

As Cox led them to the nearest

HAZMAT truck, where they were fitted with respirators, Gus said: 'Anyone see what happened?'

'Nothing concrete yet,' replied Cox. 'There were a lot of people here to see the Secretary-General. Once he'd gone the crowd started to disperse. That's when it happened.'

'And the type of gas they used . . . ?'

'Chlorine.'

'Armageddon's calling-card,' murmured Gus.

Cox nodded. 'Watch your step.'

He led them into the station and down the frozen escalators. Emergency lighting had been rigged up, and the sound of the generators echoed off the tiled walls. Everything was covered in dust and debris. Emergency personnel were working in groups, clearing debris as they went, shoring up the cracked ceilings with scaffolding poles and wooden beams.

Gus felt his blood chill even as his temper boiled. He should have been used to this by now. It was just as he'd told Renee. Man's inhumanity to man was what his job was all about. And yet this was something no sane person ever got used to. Death and destruction on this scale . . . how did anyone believe it could further any cause?

They stepped aside while another HAZMAT team carried a body-bag toward the escalators. Another victim to be ferried to the nearest morgue, searched, identified. Another family to receive the news no one ever wants to hear. Gus thought about the way this day would go down in history, the inability of the ordinary man and woman on the street to understand the why of it all, the apprehension that would dog those same people in the days, weeks and months to come, before everything got back to normal, and the unspoken understanding that nothing would ever really be normal again, after this.

He thought of Shaguma and his fists clenched so tight that his nails almost drew blood from his palms.

In the poor light, the platform where the trains had collided was barely recognizable. Twisted, wrenched and torn-apart railway cars were spilled this way and that along its entire length, casting weird, distorted shadows in every direction. The bodies of the victims who had been swept away by the sudden rush of derailed carriages had been draped in thin plastic sheets to restore a little of the dignity Shaguma had stolen from them. Gus blinked rapidly for a moment and swallowed hard. His feelings locked down tight, he told himself it was time to go to work.

'The driver of the second train,' he asked. 'What do we know about him?'

'Ordinary family man.'

'No connection with Armageddon?'

'No obvious one. And I don't believe we'll find one. I'll tell you what we *have* found, though — a second body in what's left of the driver's cab.'

'Can London Underground account for that?'

'No.'

'So it could be we're looking at a cult member who hijacked the train.'

'Looks like.'

'Okay,' said Gus. He took one final glance around. 'You fellers have got your work cut out here, and all I'm doing is slowing you down. Can I borrow one of your offices, Nick? I need someplace where I can start putting all this together.'

'Sure. I'll phone ahead and tell them to expect you.'

'Thanks. The minute you get anything — CCTV footage, any significant witness statements, forensics, anything at all — you get them to me ASAP.'

'You'll get it,' said Williams, adding grimly: 'The bastards have fucked with the wrong country this time.'

★ ★ ★

Britain held her breath in the wake of the attack, fearing that another blow might be imminent. But nothing more happened. Evidently Shaguma considered that one catastrophe was enough, at least for the moment.

The country entered a state of shock, disbelief and anger. Television coverage was constant. The media demanded that Britain be given her own Department of Homeland Security, and that a reward system be established to help bring the terrorists to book. The Prime Minister appeared on all channels to assure the people that they were safe but should under no circumstances relax their vigilance. The guilty would be found and punished, he said. But he didn't give any indication as to how long that might take.

Night fell, and in his boxy little office at Scotland Yard's Counter-Terrorism Command, Gus tried to make sense out of all the intelligence as it began to trickle in.

CCTV footage recorded at Lancaster Gate station showed a man wearing a *Transport for London* uniform and white-framed sunglasses tapping on the window of the driver's cab and then being allowed inside. Frame by frame analysis of CCTV footage recorded at the entrance to Marble Arch station was able to pick out two more people wearing the same kind of sunglasses. One appeared to be a businessman — dark-skinned, about thirty. The other looked like a construction worker — big, white, of indeterminate age. Forensics identified the remnants of a lunchbox as a container for one of the chlorine bombs. The lunchbox the construction worker had been carrying.

Witness statements began to arrive. Several people remembered seeing a priest in white sunglasses outside the station as Secretary-General Kimani's motorcade went by.

The shattered remains of a modified boom-box were identified as being another chlorine-bomb container. CCTV footage eventually tied the boom-box to a tall Goth who had entered Marble Arch station shortly before the terrorist attack was launched. More footage showed him leaving the station a few minutes later. It was no coincidence that a blonde woman in a business suit and white-framed sunglasses was walking a few steps ahead of him.

Outside, the larger open-plan office was bustling as members of the CTC — including off-duty personnel who'd fought their way back into work to lend a hand — tried to piece everything together. Facts were gathered, collated, sifted, and Nick Williams made his own stab at fitting all the pieces together without much success.

Tired and frustrated, he went outside to get a cup of tea from the machine by the elevators, and that was where he saw a tall attractive redhead who looked somewhat lost. He hadn't seen her before, so he said: 'Can I help you?'

'I'm looking for Gus Novacek,' Renee said.

'And you are . . . ?'

'Renee Forester,' she said. 'We're . . . uhm . . . friends. Close friends.'

Suspecting she might actually be a reporter trying to get an exclusive for her paper, he said: 'I'm surprised he's never mentioned you. *I* certainly would have.'

'Gus is a very private man.'

'Tell me about it. I bought him Guinness for six months before he finally told me he didn't like it. Have you got some identification, Ms. Forester?'

She showed him her pilot's license. He raised his eyebrows, then said: 'My apologies — *Captain* Forester. Come this way.'

★ ★ ★

101

Gus, meanwhile, had turned his attention to Shaguma's repeated use of chlorine gas. What had happened here was almost a carbon copy of what Shaguma had orchestrated on the Tokyo subway eight months earlier, except for the train collision. Perhaps he'd try it again on the Paris Metro, or the New York City subway. Or maybe he'd select any one of a billion other targets next time, and cause a billion times more devastation.

Chlorine gas . . . It had first been used as a weapon in World War I. If the dose was large enough, it could immobilize and kill within minutes. It had been outlawed in 1925 and again in 1992, but it was so easy to obtain that it was always going to be the fanatic's weapon of choice.

Getting the chlorine was easy, but a successful chlorine bomb attack was dependent on a number of factors, not least of which was the construction of the bomb itself. Too much explosives and the gas would be consumed by the explosion. So the key to success was to get the balance *just* right, so that the explosion breached the chlorine gas container and allowed the gas to be released . . . and that took a real craftsman — someone who might just be known to one or more of the world's law enforcement agencies.

As he was making a note to follow that up he heard a soft rapping at the door and turned in his swivel chair, expecting to see Williams.

Instead he saw Renee.

They looked at each other for a long moment, whole conversations bouncing back and forth between them until she finally said: 'Hope you don't mind. I mean, I know you're busy and everything but . . . I was worried about you.'

He stood up and motioned for her to come in and close the door. He didn't know whether or not she expected him to kiss her. After the way they'd parted it hardly seemed appropriate. 'I'm sorry,' he said. 'I should've called, but I didn't think you'd want to hear from me again.'

'I don't *think* I'd like that,' she said. Then: 'Are you any closer to nailing them?'

'Not yet. It's too soon for that. But

103

CTC's got everything in hand. The minute they find something, they'll let me know, and then I'll work it from my end.'

'Your end?'

He nodded. 'I've made a decision, Ren, and I'm flying back to New York tonight to do something about it.'

'Oh?' she said carefully.

'I always thought SENTINEL would be the one to nail Shaguma,' he said, 'but I see now that it's never going to happen that way. We're still too small, and we don't have the resources. So I'm going to liaise with just about everyone else we've got over there — the NIC, the NRO, DIA, FBI, NSA, Homeland Security, the works — and we'll find and finish Shaguma *together*.'

She showed him a quirky smile. 'It wasn't quite the weekend we hoped it would be, was it?'

'No. And I'm really sorry, Kitten. You don't know *how* sorry.'

'Want a ride to the airport?' she asked.

'Sure. And since we're still on speaking terms, I'll even buy you dinner on the way.'

'This is your idea of dinner?' she asked.

They were in the McDonald's on Mondial Way, within sight of Heathrow Airport, and Gus's own hamburger lay uneaten in its carton before him. He didn't even know why he'd ordered it. He had no appetite. The memories of what he'd seen earlier at Marble Arch were still too fresh for that.

'I'll make it up to you in New York,' he said.

'And what then, Gus? We just carry on as usual, grabbing the odd day or weekend here and there, whenever we can?'

He didn't need this after the day he'd had. 'Why do you think I want to marry you?' he said.

' "To chase away all the bad stuff," ' she quoted.

His jaw tightened. 'I told you that was only part of it.'

'Well, you were wrong, Gus. That's *all* of it.' She leaned forward over the table. 'Do you *really* think you can make all the bad stuff easier to handle just by getting married?'

'Can it make it any *worse?*'

'You know what I think? I think you've forgotten why you do your job at all.'

'Believe me, honey, there's no way I'm likely to forget some of the stuff I saw today.'

'Of course there's not. But what you saw today, Gus, what you saw up there on the Eiffel Tower, they're the *consequences*. What you need to focus on is *why* you do the job, not what happens if you don't.'

'And why's that?' he asked sullenly.

'To keep all the decent, hard-working, innocent people in the world safe, so they don't end up like all those poor souls who died today. It's for people like *me*. People like our *baby*, if we ever had one. To give us a decent shot at the future.'

She might have said more, but she'd become too emotional. Tears welled in her eyes, and seeing her like that on a shitty day like this was almost too much for Gus.

'Don't . . . please . . .'

She took a tissue from her purse, wiped her eyes.

'Kitten,' he went on helplessly, 'look, I've gotta go or I'll miss my flight. But let's talk about it in New York, huh? When are you flying back?'

'Monday.'

'I'll call you,' he said, reluctantly rising and grabbing his traveling bag. He hesitated briefly, then bent and kissed her cheek. She didn't respond.

'I'll call you,' he repeated.

When she made no reply, he turned and left the restaurant.

Part Three

New York

8

In New York, Gus started setting up meetings with the various intelligence agencies, but quickly realized that it wasn't something that he was going to be able to organize in five minutes. As much as he wanted to formulate a plan of action and move against Shaguma and Armageddon immediately, it was going to take time to agree and then coordinate such a concerted effort.

In his spartanly-furnished, one-bedroom apartment in The Village, he did a lot of thinking about the last conversation he'd had with Renee. She was right, of course. Somewhere along the line he'd lost focus, allowed the consequences of Armageddon's attacks to dominate his thoughts and bring him down. She was right about the other thing, too. It might sound corny, but it was true; he did what he did to make the world a safer place for all the Renees and Gus Juniors out there.

Late on Monday night he called Renee to tell her as much, but evidently she decided not to pick up. He tried again on Tuesday morning but still she ignored him. Maybe she was in the shower, so he left a message . . . but she never get back to him.

It was early on a miserable, wet Thursday morning when he climbed the steps to Café Lalo on West 83rd Street, flopped into a window seat and ordered Irish oatmeal and coffee. Around him the place was filled with the usual chattering or text-sending breakfast crowd.

The coffee came first, then the oatmeal, with extra raisins and hazelnuts, and as he fiddled idly with the meal a man suddenly came up behind him and laid big, long-fingered hands on his shoulders.

'Don't turn around, Novacek.'

Gus stiffened. 'Do we know each other, friend?'

'No,' said the other. 'And I'm *not* your friend.'

'So what do you want?'

'It's not what *I* want. It's what *you* want.'

112

'Which is . . . ?'

'Shaguma.'

Gus stared straight ahead, hoping to get a glimpse of the other man in the plate glass directly in front of him, but it was impossible. 'Why would I want him?' he asked at last.

'Oh, come on. No fuckin' games. I've done my homework. You want Shaguma and I can deliver him to you.'

Gus stirred the oatmeal slowly. 'How?'

'First, there's something *I* want.'

'I'm listening.'

'My kid's dying in a shithole hospital in London. He's got maybe two years left. I want him moved to someplace nice — someplace they'll treat him good.'

Gus didn't even have to think about it. 'Done.'

'An attorney will call you. When I know my kid's been taken care of, I'll give you Shaguma.'

'How do I know you can do it?'

'You don't. You're gonna have to go with your gut.' He paused to let that sink in, then said: 'Now, I'm gonna leave, and if you don't keep your eyes on your breakfast, I'll kill you and then I'll do your pilot girlfriend, too. *Comprende?*'

Gus's stomach clenched. The man knew about Renee. He *had* done his homework, then — whoever he was.

A moment later the man walked out. Gus kept staring down at his oatmeal for a long time afterward.

★ ★ ★

Rick Tanaba, Gus's normally-deskbound admin assistant at SENTINEL, found him in the rock-climbing room at the back of the K-2 Mountaineering Store later that afternoon. The room was about as large as a handball court, with a padded floor. At the far end stood an automated ten-foot rock-climbing wall, its surface pocked and studded with numerous toughened-rubber hand- and footholds. Gus, dressed in gray sweats, was climbing the wall, his chalk-covered hands moving quickly and confidently up the constantly descending surface.

'Why can't you play golf like everybody else?' called Rick. He was a bright, articulate Asian in his late twenties, short and slim, with glossy buzz-cut black hair and narrow-framed glasses, and right now he was carrying a Manila envelope. 'With golf we could've had a nice lunch at a country club. And you wouldn't stink of Ben-Gay.'

'I like the smell of Ben-Gay,' said Gus, shaking sweat out of his eyes. 'Besides, I do my best thinking while I'm climbing.' He glanced down at Rick and said: 'What have you got for me?'

'I've set up a deal with the attorney. Your guy's name is Paige Cotton.'

Gus dropped down off the wall, dried his hands on a towel and then took the envelope Rick offered him. It contained a photograph of Cotton. It showed a tall man in a T-shirt and jeans. He had long fair hair, a serious face, pocked cheeks, a square jaw, icy blue eyes.

'This is an old picture,' Gus noted.

'It's all we've got.'

'What about his son?'

'Alexander,' said Rick. 'He's got an inoperable brain tumor. We're moving him to a clinic outside Geneva.' He nodded at the photograph. 'You want the man who builds the bombs? My money's on this guy. He's a brilliant engineer and a world-class sociopath, but he must really love that boy.'

Gus shrugged. 'Go figure.'

'So what happens now?'

'We've kept our end of the deal. Now it's up to Cotton to keep *his*.'

* * *

Cotton sat on a bench in Central Park Zoo, cell phone to his ear, and watched the children in the Enchanted Forest — a large net-covered aviary — screaming and pointing at all the birds flying overhead. Just outside the aviary more children were happily climbing all over a larger-than-life spider's web. Cotton smiled as he watched them.

'The deal's done,' said his attorney, Gregory Stanfield.

'Is there any way they can weasel out?' Cotton asked.

'Not as long as you deliver your end.'

Cotton didn't reply immediately, but

the pause was only for dramatic effect. He was like one of his own detonators. Once you flicked the switch there was no going back. 'Okay,' he said. 'Let them sweat for a while — say, till tomorrow morning. Then make the call.'

★ ★ ★

Friday morning.

On the third-floor of a faded apartment on the corner of West 21st Street and Mermaid Avenue, twenty-five Armageddon cultists were seated around a large computer screen. To one side of the screen Carla Knights, a twenty-seven year-old black woman with straightened, shoulder-length hair, tapped in some instructions and a three-dimensional image of recently-completed Meadowland Stadium in East Rutherford, New Jersey, came up. As the graphic rotated, showing all the levels and exits of the stadium, Koji Shaguma ran his black eyes across his acolytes and drew pleasure from what he saw there. They were absolutely transfixed by the image on screen, in thrall of both the plan and the man behind it — the man who had been safely on his way to America by private plane even before the gas attack on London was launched.

'God has spoken to me,' he said in his deceptively gentle tone. 'He brought us here to punish America.' His eyes sought and found those of Raul Iara, in the front row. 'Will there be gas at every level?'

'Yes, Master.'

'At every level and every exit,' added Wayne Mason, who was seated next to him.

On the monitor the graphic continued to rotate, tiny lights blinking to indicate the position of the gas bombs in the exits.

At the keyboard, Carla punched up a second graphic and said: 'We've also gained access to a plane that will spray gas on the people in the stands and on the field.'

Shaguma watched the graphic, which was an aerial view of Meadowland and, just beyond it, the Meadowlands Sports Complex. It immediately cut to a side view, showing a small plane diving over the stadium's field and stands, gas fumes spewing from it.

'We've put an additive in the gas, so it won't disperse as easily as it has in the past,' Mason explained.

Shaguma nodded. 'Excellent. No one must leave the stadium alive.'

'Everything will be as you wish, Master,' Raul assured him.

Shaguma bowed to his audience, then strode imperiously from the room and headed for his personal quarters on the floor below.

* * *

About ten miles south, in a rented warehouse overlooking the Brooklyn Naval Yard, Erika Sandor was supervising a hive of activity as cult-members weighed out chemicals or assembled trigger devices and fitted them to everything from backpacks and briefcases to fanny packs and shoulder-bags. Aldo Monte was also watching them from the corner of the room, where he was talking on his cell phone.

'We'll be ready,' he said, then ended the call. He caught Erika's eye and said: 'Tomorrow. Meadowland Stadium.'

Erika nodded and smiled.

They both turned as the door opened and Cotton strolled inside, chewing on a slice of pepperoni and double-cheese pizza. He crossed to the TV in the corner and switched it on, then started surfing until he found a cartoon.

'What are you doing here?' snapped Aldo.

Cotton threw him a dismissive glance. 'What does it look like?'

'You're supposed to be with His Holiness,' said Erika.

Cotton only shrugged. 'I've been going over the trigger mechanisms in my head. I'm worried about the new relays.'

As if to confirm as much, he went to the bench where the other cultists were working on the trigger mechanisms. Cotton picked one up and examined it, aware of Aldo's suspicious scrutiny.

'They worked fine in London,' said the Italian.

'No they didn't. We had two misfires.

We're in the open this time, pal. I wanna make sure they *all* go off.'

He handed his half-chewed slice of pizza to Erika. Caught off-guard, she took it automatically. Then he picked up two mechanisms, fiddled with them until both gave a satisfactory click. When he selected a third one, however, nothing happened and he slammed it down hard on the bench, making the cultist there flinch.

Turning to Aldo and Erika he said smugly: 'Which one of you two fuckin' *devotees* wants to explain failure to the Master?' When neither replied, he said: 'Thought so . . .'

He took back his pizza and returned his attention to the cartoon on TV.

★   ★   ★

By late afternoon officers of the New York Police Department Emergency Service Unit had moved in and blocked off West 21st Street and Mermaid Avenue. Within sight of the faded glory that was once Coney Island, the neighborhood was now rundown and relatively easy to secure.

Inside the lead blue and white ESU Radio Emergency Patrol (REP) vehicle parked half a block away, Gus sat beside the officer in charge of the operation, Lieutenant Anthony Alessandro, and watched as two black Bulldog FX armored trucks crept closer to the target — Shaguma's suspected safe-house. A light but persistent drizzle tapped on the REP's roof as one Bulldog parked slantwise across West 21st and the other parked slantwise across Mermaid. ESU personnel in black Nomex jumpsuits, body armor and IIIA Magnum tactical helmets poured out of both vehicles and quickly surrounded their objective.

The house itself was nondescript, much longer than it was wide, with a flat roof and walls that were painted a dull shade of coral. A silver Dodge Caravan was parked in the yard behind the property, reflecting itself in the large puddle beneath its front wheels. Across the street stood an empty brownstone warehouse.

In the dull afternoon light Gus watched as the ESU officers dispersed, weapons in hand. Some entered the properties around the target and took up position at second-floor windows. Others kept going until they reached flat roofs and other vantage points. Then his attention turned to two more, who carefully scanned the building with green, futuristic-looking hand-held devices about twelve inches long.

'What're they doing?' he asked.

Alessandro, a stocky forty year-old Italian-American with a slow, unhurried manner, said: 'They're scanning for chemicals or other contaminants. If your cultists make a fight of it, I want to know *exactly* what we're up against.'

The radio crackled. Alessandro snatched it up, barked: 'What've you got?'

'All clear for chemicals.'

'Well, that's somethin',' he said as he replaced the handset.

Now other officers started scanning the building, this time with long, tubular devices that Gus was more familiar with. These measured infrared radiation, and would reveal the number of people and their location inside the property based on their heat signatures.

A few moments later the radio squawked again. Alessandro said: 'Go ahead.'

'We got about thirty people in there, spread throughout the house.'

'Okay. Stand by.' He swiveled around in his seat and cocked an eyebrow at Gus. 'You good to go, Novacek?

Gus nodded.

Alessandro gave the order and the remaining vehicles — a heavy-rescue truck, two SUVs, two ambulances — all followed them slowly down toward the corner.

★ ★ ★

It was Carla Knights who noticed the silence. Traffic was a constant soundtrack to life in this part of the city, and when it suddenly faded to nothing it struck her not only as odd but also worrisome.

She got up from the computer table, hurried across the large room and looked down into Mermaid Street. It was empty; no traffic, no pedestrians.

Then she glanced left, spotted one of

the black Bulldog FX trucks creeping along the center of the street and understood why.

She sucked a breath in through clenched teeth. There was always the possibility that their safe-houses could be compromised, so she didn't panic. She simply turned back to the others and said: 'Everyone — put on your glasses and arm yourselves.'

Sheep that they were, they did exactly as she had instructed, donning their white wraparound sunglasses and then scooping automatic weapons from the stack by the door before edging toward the old sash windows that overlooked the street.

Panic overtook some of them when they saw the black-clad ESU personnel taking up positions in the buildings around them, but they held firm. The Master had always prepared them for this kind of eventuality. The law enforcement agencies of the world might be the minions of Satan, but they were never to be underestimated. The course upon which Shaguma's children were set was a divine one, and Satan would do anything to stop it. When such confrontations occurred, as inevitably they must from time to time, the Master had warned them that they could expect no mercy from their enemy and should show none in return. Any fight, he had always said, would be a fight to the death.

Raul Iara and Wayne Mason left the room and hurried down to the second floor. In this kind of situation, their duty was to see to the safety of the Master. When they reached the door on the second-floor landing, Raul knocked discreetly and entered.

Shaguma was in bed with three of his newest concubines, none of whom was above the age of fifteen. He looked up from the youngest, a dark-haired girl of perhaps twelve, his hair wild, the demented spill of it covering one half of his face.

There was no need for words. His men would never have disturbed him unless the situation was serious. He rolled off the bed, finger-brushed his hair back, straightened his white robe and walked directly to the door.

'Master!' cried the twelve year-old, quickly sitting up. 'Master, come back!'

'Yes, master!' called the naked fifteen year-old beside her. 'Don't leave us!'

'Take us with you!' said the third, a thirteen year-old black girl who was also naked.

Shaguma turned and looked at them for perhaps two heartbeats. Then he went back to the bed and gently kissed each girl on top of the head.

On his way back to the door he said to Raul: 'Send them to paradise.'

Raul looked back at the girls and then coolly emptied the clip of his Uzi SMG into them.

9

As Gus and Alessandro climbed out of Alessandro's REP, the sound of gunfire carried to them on the damp afternoon air. They quickly took cover on the far side of the REP and swapped looks. A moment later the shooting stopped.

'Do you think they might have hostages?' asked Alessandro.

'I don't think so.'

'Well, somethin's got 'em pissed.'

Gus took a look around. The ESU officers, veterans of just about everything from 9/11 on down, held their fire, awaiting instructions. He reached into the REP and helped himself to Alessandro's bullhorn.

'You in the house!' he called. 'This is the Gus Novacek of SENTINEL! You are surrounded by officers of the NYPD Emergency Services Unit and we have been authorized to use deadly force, if necessary! But there's no need for anyone

to get hurt! Do you understand me? That's *not* what we want! Throw down your weapons and come out with your hands on your head. You have ten seconds!'

Inside the apartment, Shaguma stopped at the sound of Gus's voice. Raul said urgently: 'Master, we must leave.'

Shaguma nodded. 'Bring the disks.'

Raul hurried back up to the third floor and into the briefing room. He snatched up a box of disks, then stood back and sprayed the computer itself with a string of 7.62mm bullets. The computer shattered. Satisfied with his handiwork, Raul turned to the other cultists and said: 'You must sell your lives dearly.'

The cultists, pale-faced and sober-looking, nodded grimly.

* * *

From his position behind the REP, Gus saw a movement at one of the windows. The bottom half was pushed up, and then the ugly snout of a rocket-propelled grenade-launcher poked out into the street, its green warhead sweeping back and forth in search of a target.

It came to rest on the Bulldog FX truck in the center of Mermaid Street.

Something cold grabbed at Gus's throat and he had just time enough to whisper, 'Oh Christ, no,' before the missile spat out of the weapon, a thin streak of smoke scoring the air behind it.

A second later the Bulldog vanished in an orange ball of flame. The explosion lifted it is it if weighed ounces, not tons, and then it smashed back down onto the road and tipped it sideways.

Beside him he heard Alessandro shout into his ear-mike: 'Take 'em out! Repeat — *take 'em out!*'

★ ★ ★

Even before he finished speaking the ESU personnel hit the house with everything it had. The dull *crump* of tear gas and concussion grenade launchers mixed with the stutter of Heckler & Koch MP5s, the bark of M1911 semi-automatics and the booming blast of Benelli M1 shotguns, and all at once the front and side of the coral-colored building started to fracture and pock with bullet-hits.

The cultists returned fire. Slugs from their automatic weapons stitched along the street, ripping up tarmac, running along the sides of the parked REPs, flattening tires and shattering windows.

Shaguma, Raul and Mason were hurrying down the staircase when all hell broke loose. They reached the ground floor and followed a narrow hallway to a rear door. Raul forged ahead, opened the door a crack and checked the rain-soaked yard beyond.

From the roof of the building that backed onto the yard an ESU sniper fixed Raul square into his crosshairs. He said softly into his headset: 'This is Preston. I got a suspect coming out the back door.'

At the front of the building, Gus and Alessandro swapped a glance. Each had the same thought — that it was most likely Shaguma, making his getaway while his people bought him time.

Gus grabbed his black FN-five-seven out of its shoulder rig, broke cover and headed for the back of the building, bullets clipping his heels every step of the way.

Having satisfied himself that the coast was clear, Raul opened the back door a little wider and then stepped out into the yard.

Bad move.

The ESU sniper shot him through the forehead and he fell backward, into Mason's arms.

Mason's face went slack and he quickly drew the corpse back inside and kicked the door shut. 'What now?' he asked.

Shaguma said calmly: 'Get the car.'

Mason hesitated briefly, then nodded and threw himself out into the yard, using his own Uzi to spray the opposite rooftop while he bolted for the Dodge Caravan.

Gus came around the corner just as Mason reached the car and threw himself behind the wheel. Seconds later the snipers returned fire, their bullets shattering the windshield. Running on adrenalin now, Mason started the car, slammed it into reverse and burned rubber as he backed up to the rear door of the safe-house.

The instant the vehicle skidded to a halt, Shaguma broke cover and ran toward it. A split second later one of the snipers' bullets hit the gas tank and the car exploded.

The blast hurled Shaguma back against the building, where he slid to the ground, shards of jagged silver metal protruding from his suddenly blood-soaked chest. As Gus skirted the burning wreck and closed the last couple of yards toward him, he could see the man was dying and felt a curious kind of disappointment that, in the end, it had all been so easy.

He knelt beside the cult leader. Shaguma seemed unaware of his presence. Into his ear-mike Gus snapped: 'I need an ambulance here, *now!*'

Then all his anger spilled out and he grabbed Shaguma roughly by one shoulder. Shaguma came out of his trance and looked at him through faraway but still spiteful eyes.

His lips worked. A moment later sound came out. 'Novacek,' he managed.

Gus nodded. 'Yeah. And we nailed you after all, didn't we?'

'Y-you have only . . . hastened m-me on my . . . way to paradise.'

'You've got it all wrong, Shaguma. You're headed for hell, you miserable little prick.'

Shaguma's bearded lips twitched again, but this time no words came out. There was movement at the corner. Gus turned, brought his gun up, then relaxed as he recognized two ESU medics. Rising, he stepped back to allow them to take care of Shaguma. As he did so he spotted Raul Iara's corpse in the doorway . . . and the box of computer disks that lay next to him.

★　★　★

At the warehouse overlooking the Brooklyn Naval Yard, Aldo, Erika and the others saw it all on the TV news. One of the cultists, a tall, narrow-hipped girl with straight black hair whose name was Jasmine Bradham, sobbed uncontrollably as they watched the ESU medics load the

Master into an ambulance. An oxygen mask covered his pale face and an IV line was attached to one arm.

He looked neither invincible nor godlike.

Other images followed — of the wrecked safe-house, police leading hand-cuffed cultists toward waiting vans. Their expressions were flat, beaten.

Then the report cut to Gus and Lieutenant Alessandro holding an impromptu press conference in the rain-wet street.

'How bad is Shaguma?' asked an off-camera reporter.

'I'm not a doctor,' Gus replied vaguely.

'But does this signal the end of Armageddon's threat to the world?'

'A full statement will be made available in due course.'

Cotton worked the remote control and the TV went blank. Silence filled the large room. Then Jasmine said quietly: 'Please don't die, Your Holiness.'

With the silence broken, everyone started talking at once. *What are we going to do? We've got to rescue the Master! How did they find us, anyway? Maybe they're already on their way here!*

Cotton clapped his hands to shut them up. 'We're terrorists, people!' he growled. 'The worst thing we can do now is panic, so just shut the fuck up and let's *think* about this!'

He fell quiet and wandered across the room, then turned and stabbed a finger at Erika. 'You and me'll check the hospitals, find out where they took the Master. Aldo — you and the others set up the bombs in the stadium, okay?'

Aldo hesitated, bristling briefly at Cotton's take-charge attitude. But Cotton was right. Until they knew differently, they must assume that their attack on the Secretary-General's speech at Meadowland Stadium was still on.

★　★　★

They rushed Shaguma to Coney Island Hospital, on Ocean Parkway, where he underwent emergency surgery. When Rick Tanaba showed up about an hour later he found Gus in the seventh-floor visitor's area, just along the corridor from the

136

Surgical Intensive Care Unit.

'What the hell're you doing here?' asked Gus.

Rick held out a sandwich and a Styrofoam cup of coffee as if they were peace offerings. 'I figured you'd be hungry by now.'

'I'm not, but thanks, anyway.'

With a shrug Rick sat next to him and started to unwrap his sandwich.

'How's it going with those disks we retrieved from the safe-house?' Gus asked.

'It's not. We've tried just about everything we can think of, but their password-protected — and the password's proving to be a tough one to crack.'

'What about the woman? Carla Knights?'

She had come to Gus's attention for two reasons. During the arrest of the safe-house survivors, the cultists had looked to her for orders, which implied that she was an important cog in the Armageddon machine. A background check had also revealed that before she joined the cult, she had been a computer software analyst — apparently a pretty good one.

Rick grinned. 'She's been about as cooperative as a rattlesnake,' he said around a mouthful of pastrami.

'Damn.'

'How's he doing in there, anyway?'

'Shaguma? Touch and go.'

'And you're hoping it's go, right?'

'Straight to hell,' Gus replied, but almost immediately his face shadowed. 'And yet there's a part of me that knows it's not gonna be over even when this bastard dies.'

'Why not?'

'Because Shaguma's chief lieutenants are gonna do whatever they can to get even.'

Rick paused. 'So the war goes on, huh?'

'The war goes on,' Gus confirmed softly.

* * *

Night.

Cotton and Erika sat in an old Ford Explorer just across the street from the hospital emergency zone. It stood to reason that the authorities would take the Master to the closest hospital, and CIH was barely five minutes from the safehouse on Mermaid, so Cotton drove then there first.

As they parked he said: 'He's here.'

Erika frowned. 'How do you know?'

'Look over there,' he said, indicating the distinctive white and blue markings of two NYPD Emergency Service Units in front of the hospital. 'Who else would have the balls to park in an emergency zone? And take a look just inside the foyer.'

She did, and saw two uniformed police officers standing guard.

'How are we going to get past them?'

'I'll figure something out,' he said.

In the distance they heard the wailing of a siren, getting closer. Less than a half a minute later an ambulance swerved into the emergency zone and the paramedics leapt out. They opened the rear doors and pulled out a patient on a gurney. Orderlies ran out of the hospital to help wheel the patient into the ER.

Cotton grinned in the darkness. 'That's what we need,' he said. 'An *emergency.*'

He quickly leaned over and clamped one hand across Erika's mouth. Instinctively she began to struggle, her blue eyes wide with shock. A second later she froze as Cotton drove his knife into her stomach.

He looked directly into her eyes, which were wide and filled with pain. 'Don't die on me *yet*, sweetheart,' he whispered.

★   ★   ★

The Emergency Room was frantic. Doctors, nurses and orderlies were all doing their best to whittle down the apparently endless stream of waiting patients. As Cotton carried Erika inside, it was all he could do not to smile. In this kind of chaos, what he had planned should be child's play.

'Somebody!' he yelled. 'I need help, here! Please!'

As soon as he got the attention of the nearest nurses and orderlies, the massive bloodstain across Erika's stomach did the

140

rest. They came running, and carefully took her from him.

'What happened?' asked a nurse.

Feigning shock, Cotton mumbled: 'My girl . . . she's been stabbed . . . '

As they placed Erika on a gurney she opened her mouth and tried to talk, but blood choked off whatever she was trying to say. She pointed weakly at Cotton, who immediately grabbed her hand and started stroking it.

'It's okay, baby. Don't try to talk.'

They wheeled her away then, toward one of the operating rooms, and Cotton went after them, still feigning confusion. 'We were just walking along and this . . . this gang-banger grabbed her purse. I tried to stop him but the sonofabitch stabbed her and . . . and — '

An orderly blocked his path into the operating room. 'You can't go in there, bud.'

Cotton nodded and watched through the window as an ER doctor and a team of nurses began the fight to save Erika's life. Although the doctor made repeated attempts to resuscitate her, it was useless.

He finally pulled a sheet over Erika's face, looked through the window at Cotton and shook his head.

Playing his part to the hilt, Cotton clapped one hand across his eyes and swayed as if he were about to collapse. The orderly immediately grabbed him and led him to a chair. 'You stay right here, buddy,' he instructed. 'I'll go find a cop for you.'

Cotton nodded numbly.

He waited until the orderly was out of sight, then stood up and headed for the elevators. He rode up to the first floor, then hurried along the corridor until he found what he was looking for — a room marked HOSPITAL STAFF ONLY.

10

The room had only one occupant, a nurse enjoying a cup of coffee before a TV set with the volume turned low. Cotton closed the door softly behind him, saw footage of the new United Nations Secretary-General visiting a children's home in Union City.

'This morning, Secretary-General Kimani took a few moments out of his busy schedule to do the thing he loves most . . . comfort needy children. This is truly a remarkable man — without doubt one of the most revered human beings alive . . . '

Hearing him behind her, the nurse turned. Not missing a beat he grinned at her, grabbed a jacket marked HOSPITAL VOLUNTEER off the coat rack beside the door and then left.

He made a quick study of the hospital map beside the elevators and then rode up to the Surgical ICU. When he stepped out onto the seventh floor he immediately spotted two police officers standing watch outside a room halfway along the corridor. That's where they were holding Shaguma, then — he'd put money on it.

He was just about to start toward them when two other men appeared from the visitor's area at the far end. He recognized Gus immediately. He was accompanied by a shorter man, Asian, maybe Chinese. Cotton automatically scooped up a bowl of flowers from the nurse's station and then turned and walked in the opposite direction.

Directly ahead lay an open door, beyond which he could see a dark-haired boy of about nine stretched out in a bed, watching TV. He went straight in, set the bowl down and said: 'You're up late, buddy.'

'Can't sleep,' said the boy. He had a pale face, dark, sunken eyes.

Cotton picked up the chart at the end of the bed, saw that the boy's name was Daniel Nelson, that he had been admitted for nerve pain associated with his paraplegia. 'Anything I can do for you, Danny?' he asked cheerfully.

The boy shrugged. 'The remote's broken. I can't change channels.'

Cotton went to the wall-mounted TV and manually worked his way through the channels until he came to an old re-run of *BraveStarr*. 'How about that?' he asked.

'Cool.'

Cotton dragged a chair over to the boy's bedside, positioning it so that he could see out the door and into the mezzanine area in front of the elevators. Then he grinned at the boy and said: 'Man, I *love* cartoons.'

★ ★ ★

Shaguma lay in a post-operative coma. A life support system was doing everything for him, but the monitors confirmed the truth of the situation — that despite the best efforts of his surgeons, he was barely clinging to life.

When the life-support alarms started beeping, Gus and Rick came running. By then a doctor and nurses were already in the room, trying to resuscitate the cult leader. Gus watched them from the doorway, knowing it was useless. And sure enough, five minutes later the team stopped working and the doctor came outside.

'I'm sorry,' he said.

'I'm not,' replied Gus.

But he hadn't wanted it to end like this. He'd wanted Shaguma to stand trial for his crimes and be exposed to his followers for the charlatan he was. Now that he was dead and beyond any form of justice, he would become a martyr to them, and they would do whatever it took to make the rest of the world pay for his loss.

He watched the nurses inside the ICU disconnect Shaguma from the life support system, and suddenly frowned. 'Tell them to keep him hooked up,' he said.

The doctor frowned at him. 'Excuse me? The guy's already dead.'

'Sure he is. But nobody has to know that yet, do they?'

'Are you crazy? I can't keep a *corpse* in ICU!'

'Yes, you can. I want everyone to think he's alive.'

'Look, I don't think you understand — '

'No — *you* don't understand, doc. I work for the President. Got it? Now, get in there and keep him hooked up!' As the doctor went back into the room, shaking his head, Gus turned to the cops standing guard. 'Nobody gets in. And if anybody finds out that he's dead, it'll be your badges.'

He started up the corridor toward the elevators, Rick hurrying to match his stride. 'What's going on?' he asked. 'Shaguma's dead. Why keep that under wraps?'

'I want you to go get the Knights woman,' Gus said, glancing left and seeing a hospital volunteer sitting beside a sick kid in a bed, watching TV.

'You mean bring her here?'

'That's it.'

'Why?'

'You'll find out,' Gus said.

★ ★ ★

He was waiting outside Shaguma's room when Rick brought Carla Knights up to

147

the Surgical ICU. The tall, lithe black woman was flanked by two thickset SENTINEL agents in suits and ties. Carla wore the same sullen look that Gus had seen countless times before. She wanted them to think she wasn't scared but he could tell by her eyes that she was. No one had told her why they'd brought her here — no one other than Gus knew. And the uncertainty was killing her resistance, though she was trying hard to fight it.

When she saw Gus waiting for her she yelled: 'How long before you let me talk to my lawyer?'

'That's up to you,' he said.

'Meaning?'

'I need the password to your computer files.'

'Fuck you.'

Gus shrugged. 'All right, Carla. Have it your own way.'

He glanced through the window in the door, and Carla followed it automatically. Inside the room she saw Shaguma lying in bed, hooked up to life-support systems that had been carefully reset to respond as if the cult leader were still alive.

'I'll make this easy,' he said. 'Give me the password or I'll pull the plug on Shaguma.'

'You're bluffing.'

He moved so fast she didn't even see it coming, and fastened the fingers of his right hand tight around her throat.

Rick said, 'Gus . . . ' but Gus ignored him.

'No, Carla,' he said. 'What I am is sick and tired of shitheads like you, spreading fear and death because you think it's gonna buy you a place in paradise. So I'm gonna play you at your own game.'

Her eyes narrowed warily.

Without another word he released his grip on her and entered ICU. Carla watched his every movement. He went directly to the life-support system and very deliberately disconnected it. Instantly, the monitor displaying Shaguma's fake heartbeat started to beep and the lifeline went flat.

Carla went berserk. She struggled against the agents that held her, but couldn't break their grip on her manacled arms.

'You fucking maniac!' she screamed. 'Put it back!'

'When he gets the password,' said Rick, as understanding finally dawned.

Emotion warred in Carla's expression, love for Shaguma, loyalty to the cause, hatred for Gus and everything he represented.

Love won.

'ZERO!' she spat. 'Now, do it! Do it!'

Gus ignored her and came out of ICU. She couldn't believe he could show the same disregard for life that she and her fellow cultists practiced on a daily basis.

'You fucking murderer!' she shouted. 'You've killed *god!*'

Not once taking his eyes off her face, he said: 'A piece of metal two feet long killed your *god*, lady. He died thirty minutes ago.'

* * *

'Erika's dead?' asked Aldo. 'How?'

By the time Cotton had returned to the warehouse it was almost two in the morning. Having decided with each

150

passing minute that they were safe from discovery, at least for now, the cultists had finally relaxed enough to pray for the Master or gradually doze off.

Cotton's arrival had reawakened their panic. He had never realized just how good at panic they were. Except for Aldo, of course. Aldo was always calm and collected. But Cotton was pleased to see that his news had even rattled the Italian.

'Want me to draw you a fucking picture?' he said. 'The cops shot her.'

'How come you're still alive?'

'Erika saved my nuts. I never liked that bitch, but I gotta give her credit. She took a bullet in the tits so I could sneak into the hospital.'

Jasmine Bradham came forward. 'What about His Holiness?'

'They were wheeling him out of ICU when I got there,' he lied easily. 'I couldn't get close enough to see how he was, but he was definitely awake.'

Jasmine swayed a little with relief.

Aldo checked the time. 'Ten hours from now, Meadowlands stadium will turn into a cemetery. That's when we'll

151

bust the Master out of hospital.'

His head snapped around at Cotton's harsh bark of laughter.

'What's so funny?'

'You. How the *fuck* did you get to be so stupid, Aldo? There's a million cops at the hospital.'

'*You* got in.'

'Yeah, but you're not me. Besides, I got in *alone*. And at the cost of Erika. Still, you go ahead. But you can count me out.'

Aldo squared up to him. 'You'll do exactly as I say.'

'Or what?' countered Cotton. 'You'll shoot me?'

Jasmine broke the moment. 'What if we don't hit the hospital?'

'I'll find a way to get the Master out and everybody'll be safe,' said Cotton.

As Jasmine and the other cultists looked uncertainly at each other, Cotton saw yet again just how easy it had been for Shaguma to get the Armageddon movement started. These people had no ambition, no drive. They were sheep. All they wanted was for someone to tell them what to do, because it was easier than having to decide for themselves.

Finally Jasmine looked at Aldo and said: 'Maybe it wouldn't hurt to listen.'

Knowing that Cotton had won them over, Aldo could only shrug as if it were no big deal. But when he turned back to Cotton there was ice in his tone. 'If anything goes wrong, you won't have to worry about the cops,' he said softly. 'I'll kill you *myself.*'

★   ★   ★

It was the middle of the morning by the time Gus and Rick arrived back at SENTINEL's suite of offices in the Manhattan Municipal Building on Chambers Street. It had been a long Friday and an even longer Friday night into Saturday morning, what with the ESU debriefing Gus had been required to attend. Both men were dead on their feet, but they still had work to do. Rick flopped into the chair behind his paper-littered desk, slipped the first of the Armageddon disks into his computer, then typed in

ZERO and hit *Enter*.

'Fuck,' he whispered.

The message on the screen said *ACCESS DENIED*.

'Try it as a numeral,' said Gus.

Rick hit *0* on the keyboard and said: 'I'm in!'

Gus leaned a little closer. On screen, he saw a 3D graphic of some kind of stadium. He narrowed his eyes at it. 'You recognize that place?'

Rick scanned the screen. 'There's nothing to say where it is . . . only the date. *Today*'s date.' he muttered. He used his mouse to turn the image around, to zoom in and then zoom out.

The moment he saw the second stadium above the first Gus recognized it. 'It's the new Meadowlands stadium in New Jersey!'

'Are you sure?'

'Sure enough. It lies right next to the Meadowlands Sports Complex.'

Behind his glasses, Rick's eyes narrowed. 'The 'Big M'?'

'That's it.'

'Okay. We've got a date and we've got a

location. But it's these blinking red lights that worry me.'

The lights Rick was referring to appeared to highlight specific points in and around the stadium. 'They're planning a gas attack on Meadowlands,' said Gus. 'But that doesn't make sense. There's no football out there tonight.'

'No,' Rick confirmed. 'But there's a rally for the UN Secretary-General!'

'When?'

Rick checked his watch. 'In about thirty minutes' time.'

'Jesus!' Gus snatched up the phone. 'Get me the new Meadowlands stadium security office — *now!*'

★   ★   ★

It didn't take long, but it used up precious minutes they couldn't afford to waste. At last a voice came on the line. 'Bernie Thomason, chief of security. Who's this?'

'Novacek, SENTINEL. Listen, Thomason, we've got reason to believe that you've been targeted for a terrorist attack,

155

and I need you to get Joseph Kimani out of there and start evacuating the stadium immediately.'

There was an intake of breath at the other end of the line. 'You have any idea what you're asking?'

'Don't argue with me, dammit, just *do* it!'

He slammed the phone down and turned to Rick, who was already on the other line. 'I need a — '

'I know,' said Rick. 'A chopper. Better get up to the roof, Gus. It'll be here any minute.'

* * *

The stadium's three tiers, which were capable of holding more than 82,000 spectators, had already started filling up. In the center of the field stood a podium from which Joseph Kimani would address his audience. More people were already clustered around the stadium, heading for the turnstiles only to be turned away by security personnel.

The NYPD Bomb Squad had already

arrived. EDCs — Explosive Detection Canines — and their handlers were being deployed to begin a thorough search of the stadium. Matt black bomb containers were unloaded and carried inside by bomb squad officers. Their orders were clear — there was no time to dufuse the bombs. The priority was to seal them up and deal with them later.

* * *

Bernie Thomason intercepted the Secretary-General and his entourage. He caught up with them in the tunnel leading out to the playing field.

'I'm sorry, Mr. Secretary. There's been a bomb threat. We have to get you and your staff out of the stadium.'

Joseph Kimani's light brown eyes, flecked with gold, moved briefly toward the field ahead of them. 'But what about all the people?'

'They're being evacuated, sir. Now please, come this way.'

* * *

Bomb Squad personnel found the first device half-buried in a trash barrel. After making a quick check for booby traps, they sealed it into one of the bomb containers. A second device was found less than ten minutes later, and removed from a seemingly discarded hamburger box. This too was sealed into a container.

Two down.

The search went on.

* * *

The flight across New York in the commandeered FBI ASTAR AS350B2 took less than twenty minutes. Gus received updates every step of the way. Then as the New Jersey Turnpike appeared ahead and below Rick reported a new and potentially chilling development.

'The FAA's just picked up an unauthorized flight over the area, a two-seater Zenair Zodiac XL, bright yellow in color. All attempts at radio contact have failed — the pilot's just not answering. His flight path seems erratic, too. He's flying around the area of the stadium, but not really going anywhere.'

'What's the FAA done about it?' Gus asked into his headset.

'They've scrambled to two Raptors from Mitchel AFB.'

Just then the pilot nudged him and he looked up. 'I see the plane,' he said into the headset. It was a light aircraft with a long, clear-Plexiglas canopy covering the cockpit. He grabbed a pair of binoculars and gave the aircraft a searching sweep, focusing particularly on the pilot and his passenger.

The pilot and passenger who were both wearing white-framed wraparound sunglasses.

He swallowed, then said: 'They're cultists, Rick. I say again — they're cultists.'

The scrambled aircraft — two gray F22 Raptors — dove out of nowhere, their twin afterburners glowing orange as they overtook the Zodiac and then came back around in another gliding dive through the blue afternoon sky. As the helicopter settled to a hover over the stadium, Gus could imagine what was happening there now. The pilots would be making one final stab at contacting the Zodiac, issuing a warning and an opportunity to withdraw or cease threatening action.

The Zodiac dropped lower and came back around to overfly the stadium one more time. As it did so something began to drift from its undercarriage, a thick white mist that began to spread and drift slowly but steadily to earth.

Chlorine gas.

'Get us out of here!' said Gus. The pilot pulled on the collective and the chopper tilted violently and then angled out of the line of fire.

The lead Raptor swooped on the Zodiac and weapons bays opened on each side of its fuselage. A second later two short-range missiles streaked forward and blew the Zodiac apart. The chopper yawed drunkenly, caught in the blast's shockwave, and then steadied again. Gus turned in his seat to watch what was left of the Zodiac — little more than flaming debris now — tumble to earth.

* * *

At the warehouse Cotton, Aldo and the others watched in dismay as Gus addressed the assembled news media outside the stadium. In a fit of rage, Aldo kicked the set in and then whirled around to confront Cotton and the other cultists.

'We'll make those fuckers pay!' he hissed. 'But first, we have to rescue The Master.' He sucked in a breath and said to Cotton: 'Okay, *sapientone*, let's hear your plan.'

11

When Cotton entered Danny Nelson's hospital room on Monday morning, once again wearing his stolen HOSPITAL VISITOR jacket and pushing a wheelchair ahead of him, he found the youngster studying a bowl of oatmeal with unbridled dismay. When he too saw the oatmeal, Cotton drew up sharp and pulled a face.

'Yuck,' he said.

'I know,' said Danny. 'It's totally gross.'

'How'd you like to have a *real* breakfast?' asked Cotton, as if the idea had suddenly occurred to him. 'Pancakes, eggs, sausage — the whole nine yards?'

The boy's face immediately brightened. 'Can we go to McDonald's?'

Cotton thought about it — for all of two seconds. 'Sure,' he grinned. 'Why not?'

★　★　★

At about the same time Aldo and Jasmine, both dressed in business suits, boarded an airport shuttle helicopter on top of the Pan Am Building, bound for Kennedy Airport. When the chopper finally took off, they exchanged a look. Then Aldo furtively slipped one hand into his zippered bag.

As he pulled out the Uzi one of the passengers screamed. But there was no time for anyone to react further: Jasmine drew a Beretta automatic from her purse and yelled: 'Everyone, stay in your seats and you won't get hurt!'

She kept everyone covered while Aldo went forward to the pilot, who was already reaching for his panic button, the one that would alert his supervisor that something up here had suddenly gone terribly wrong. He froze when Aldo pressed the Uzi's cold snout against the back of his neck.

'Just do as I say, fly-boy.'

The pilot nodded cautiously.

★ ★ ★

Cotton drove the old Ford Explorer through the heavy rush-hour traffic. Behind him, buckled up in the back seat, Danny Nelson said: 'I thought we were going to McDonald's?'

'We are,' Cotton replied without looking around. 'But before we go to McDonald's I want to take you someplace else first.'

Danny grinned and gestured to the bouquet on the seat beside him. 'To see your *girlfriend?*' he teased.

Cotton shook his head. 'To see the most powerful man in the world,' he said.

★ ★ ★

At his apartment in Greenwich Village, Gus woke late, made coffee and then tuned into CNN's live coverage of the Secretary-General's journey to Kennedy Airport, where he would embark upon the next leg of his world tour. A police motorcycle escort led the way. Next came two SUVs filled with Secret Service agents. Then came Kimani's open-topped limo, followed by one more Secret Service SUV.

Crowds lined the route to the airport. While the commentators rehashed the story of Saturday afternoon's evacuation of the Meadowlands Stadium, the camera panned the crowds.

Gus got up and rinsed his mug under the faucet. He wasn't especially interested in Kimani's visit and was only half watching when the camera focused on a ten year-old boy in a wheelchair, a bouquet of flowers on his lap. The boy's companion, a man of about thirty with short blond hair, bent and said something to him, then pointed up the street, indicating the direction from which the Secretary-General's motorcade would approach.

Gus frowned. He didn't know if it was something about the boy's companion that struck him as being familiar, or if it was some sixth sense that made him feel suddenly uneasy. He set the mug down and leaned closer to the TV. The blond man said something in the boy's ear. Gus lip-read: *Get ready. This is your big moment.*

He knew he'd seen their faces before, but he couldn't immediately place them.

He was on his way to the shower when it hit him.

Friday night — the hospital.

He'd seen the man and the boy in the boy's room as he walked Rick Tanaba to the elevators.

He hurried back to the TV, but the image had changed. It didn't matter. The blond man's face was still fixed in Gus's mind. He went over to his cluttered desk, picked up the dossier Rick had prepared on Paige Cotton and opened it. The picture might be old, but the resemblance was unmistakable.

He snatched up the phone.

★ ★ ★

As Joseph Kimani's limo drew level with them, Cotton said: 'Now, Danny. Hold the flowers nice and high, so the Secretary-General can see them.'

Caught up in the excitement of the moment, not once thinking to question why a man he had never seen before Friday evening had brought him to see this man he'd never even heard of, Danny did as he was told. Joseph Kimani swept his gaze from one side of the street to the other, waving constantly with both hands. Then his eyes settled on Danny, offering up his bouquet, and the Secretary-General said something to the Secret Service man beside him. The Secret Service man spoke to the driver and the limo stopped.

To a thunderous roar of approval, Kimani stepped out of the limo and started toward the boy.

★　★　★

The cameras were quick to capture the moment. Gus saw it unfolding even as Jason Wickes, one of the Secret Service agents assigned to Kimani's party, finally answered his cell.

'Wickes.'

'Novacek,' Gus replied tightly. 'Listen — you've got a possible hit on Kimani!'

'Who?'

'See the kid in the wheelchair? It's the guy behind him. He's one of Shaguma's zombies.'

'We're on it!'

As Kimani reached for the flowers the small chlorine bomb Cotton had secreted inside the bouquet went off, the gas immediately enveloping the Secretary-General and the boy in the wheelchair. Bystanders suddenly erupted into a screaming, yelling mob until the gas got to them and then the screams and yells turned to coughs and gasps.

Cotton stepped backward just before the bomb went off, turned and pulled a protective half-face filter mask out of his jacket pocket and quickly snapped it on. A pair of protective goggles came next — and then a Colt semi-automatic.

Before the Secret Service agents could reach him, a dozen other cultists who'd infiltrated the crowd also donned respirators and goggles and pulled out a variety of weapons of their own. They stepped forward and quickly gunned the agents down.

Chaos immediately ensued, and to make things even worse, some of the cultists started throwing additional gas bombs into the crowd.

* * *

In the sky above, the shuttle 'copter thumped slowly into view, and Aldo signaled for the pilot to take them down.

'I can't land in the street!' the pilot argued desperately. 'Anyway, it looks like there's a fucking battle going on down there!'

Aldo shrugged, then turned and shot the nearest passenger, a forty year-old woman, between the breasts. She screamed as the 7.62mm bullets ripped her open and one leg kicked even after she was dead.

'How about now?' asked Aldo.

Sick-faced, the pilot took them down.

* * *

The street was wreathed in tear gas and littered with bodies. Bystanders were staggering blindly, coughing into handkerchiefs or dropping to their knees, hardly able to breathe. Mothers were screaming for their children and vice versa. And among all the chaos, the

169

Secret Service agents were still exchanging gunfire with the cultists.

At the sound of the first explosion the motorcycle escort had turned back to support the Secret Service agents, but the cultists had expected that. The police ran straight into a hail of gunfire and gas grenades that tore them apart. Three officers fell from their bikes and rolled into the gutter. The motorcyclists immediately behind them couldn't stop in time and collided with the fallen machines. They too went down. A bullet hit a gas tank and the explosion hurled one of the bikes high into the air before slamming it down again on top of the nearest SUV.

While all this was going on, the shuttle 'copter set down at the far end of the street. While Aldo kept an eye on the pilot, Jasmine motioned with her Beretta that the other passengers should get out. They needed no urging.

Joseph Kimani was down on his hands and knees, coughing. His eyes were on fire and he couldn't see a thing. But he could still hear, and the sounds of gunfire and screaming tore at him. People were being killed, people who had come out to see *him*, and he couldn't help but feel responsible for that. Then he heard a particularly plaintive voice nearby.

'Help me . . . please . . . please . . . '

The boy! The boy in the wheelchair, who'd been about to give him the flowers when the bomb went off!

Heedless of the battle going on around him, Kimani got to his feet. He felt sick and disoriented, but determined to help the child.

He took a single step toward the boy's voice when Cotton grabbed him and started dragging him along the street.

'Wait! *Wait!* There's a boy back there . . . he needs our help!'

There was a single shot, so close that Kimani flinched. And then Cotton's voice said: 'Not any more he doesn't.'

★ ★ ★

The minute he hung up from Wilkes, Gus had headed for his car. But any hopes he'd entertained of reaching the scene of the attack in time to lend a hand were

171

dashed by gridlocked rush-hour traffic. By the time his Dodge Charger squealed to a halt before the confusion of wrecked bikes, stalled cars and dead or dying people, the hijacked helicopter was long gone.

* * *

In the helicopter, Cotton moved forward to Aldo, who was still keeping the ashen-faced pilot covered. As Aldo glanced at him, Cotton tugged off his respirator and goggles and responded with a taunting grin.

'Still think we can't make it?' he asked.

He glanced out at the sprawl of New York below them, the greener, grayer, flatter expanse of Kennedy Airport in the distance.

He felt good. But it had been closer than he cared to admit. Of the dozen cultists who'd taken part in the abduction, seven hadn't made it to the chopper. Whether they were dead or wounded or just plain unlucky made no difference to him. His plan, *the* plan, was well underway now, and there would be no stopping it.

He returned beside Kimani. Tears were still streaking the statesman's cheeks and welling in his painful, gas-reddened eyes. 'Welcome aboard, Mr. Secretary.'

Kimani looked up blindly, and then, so fast that no one saw it coming, he lashed out and slapped Cotton's face. His aim was excellent. Enraged, Cotton raised his Colt. Kimani heard the sound he made working the slide, but showed no fear. It made Cotton's anger fade a little and suddenly he grinned, almost in respect.

'You crusty old bastard,' he said. 'Don't you know God hates violence?'

'Don't you dare bring God's name into this,' Kimani hissed.

'Jesus Christ! You sound just like my ol' man.'

Jasmine turned away from one of the chopper's windows. 'There's a helicopter following us,' she said.

Cotton leaned across Kimani and took a look for himself. He relaxed a little when he realized it was just a TV news chopper, flying parallel with them. A

173

cameraman was filming everything as they buzzed through the skies above New York.

Cotton tucked his Colt away, tore an Uzi from the hands of another cultist and then pulled the door open. He quickly took aim and fired at the other chopper. The pilot hurriedly peeled the 'copter away. Cotton laughed as he watched it go.

But as they headed toward Kennedy Airport, another helicopter, the same gray FBI ASTAR Gus had commandeered the previous Saturday, followed from a safe distance.

In the co-pilot's seat, Gus spoke into his headset. 'They're heading for Kennedy. Have Airport Security set up a command post and get some ESU teams out there ASAP.'

A few moments later a new voice crackled in Gus's ear. 'I'm talking to Novacek, right?'

'Right.'

'This is Collins, Kennedy Security. We've got your terrorists on radar. They're heading for the west end of the field.'

'Clear the area and cordon it off, Collins.'

'Way ahead of you there, buddy.'

★ ★ ★

At the western edge of the field stood a row of hangars. Outside the last of these was a Concorde SST carrying the Speedbird logo. Sitting beside Kimani, who had finally regained some of his sight, Cotton called out: 'Have the pilot put down beside that Concorde.'

Aldo glared back at him. 'Why?'

'Because we need a way out of here and that's still the fastest fucking plane on the planet, that's why,' Cotton replied.

The shuttle 'copter slowly descended toward the hangars until it joined its shadow on the tarmac.

Cotton looked out the window at a fleet of approaching police cars. He seemed immune to the tension that was now starting to affect the others. 'Aren't you gonna tell me we'll never get away with this?' he asked Kimani.

Kimani gave him a level, unwavering

stare that seemed to look right inside him. 'God's already taken care of that,' he said softly.

Cotton grinned. 'Hey, man,' he said. 'If God's my only problem, I'm home free.'

12

As the ASTAR came in to land behind the line of police cars and ESU vehicles that had surrounded the area, Gus watched the cultists leave the shuttle 'copter and head for the nearest hangar, Cotton pushing Kimani roughly ahead of him. The Secretary-General stumbled, but Cotton stopped him from falling altogether and pushed him on toward the hangar.

Sight of the Concorde nearby stirred a memory of Renee. He'd lost track of her schedule over the last week. He could only hope she was safe in London right now.

The ASTAR touched down. Gus jumped out and crouch-ran out from under the rotors. He spotted Lieutenant Alessandro beside his REP and headed toward him. As he did, his phone rang. He took it out, and without checking the caller ID said: 'Make it quick.' The caller spoke and Gus broke stride, drew a breath and said: 'I'm sorry, Mr. President. Go ahead, sir.'

'For starters,' said the President, 'what the hell's going on there?'

'Shaguma's people have abducted the Secretary-General. They've holed up in one of the hangars at the west end of Kennedy Airport.'

'Jesus Christ, Gus, he's just won the Nobel *Peace* Prize! What do they want?'

'They haven't said yet, sir.'

'Well, I've got the whole universe breathing down my neck on this. Don't be a cowboy. Just do whatever it takes to get Kimani out of there in one piece, you got that?'

'Yes, sir.'

The radio in Alessandro's REP suddenly squawked and he snatched it off its hook. 'Go ahead.'

'This is Collins, Airport Security. They've just made contact from the hangar. Shall I patch 'em through?'

'Sir, I've got to go,' said Gus. 'We're about to open a dialogue.'

Alessandro said, 'Patch 'em through,'

and passed the handset to Gus, who said: 'Novacek.'

'Do as I say,' said a voice, 'or we'll kill Kimani.'

It wasn't Cotton. The accent was clipped and businesslike, Italian. 'You got it,' Gus said. 'What do you want?'

Inside the hangar, Aldo Monte said: 'Two things: His Holiness. That SST fueled and ready to go. And no interference from you or anybody else.'

'That won't be easy,' said Gus, 'but I'll get right on it.'

'Don't give me any bullshit, Novacek. I want everything, and I want it *now*.'

'And I'd love to give it to you now. But like I say, it'll take *time*.'

'Then stop wasting what you've got.'

'There's something else,' Gus hedged carefully. 'Shaguma's badly shot up. If we move him, he might not make it.'

'If he doesn't, Joseph Kimani's dead. You've got an hour.'

The line went silent.

Gus thought quickly, then punched a number into his cell. 'Rick?' he said grimly. 'I've got a job for you.'

Rick Tanaba looked up from the gurney. His head was swathed in bandages, from which black strands of hair could just be seen. His body was hidden beneath a gray blanket. There was an IV bag attached to one arm. It wasn't perfect, Gus thought, but it would have to do.

'Well?' asked Rick. 'Will I pass for Shaguma?'

Gus tucked a handgun into Rick's right hand, then covered it with the blanket. 'Let's put it this way,' he said. 'You Asians *don't* all look alike.'

'You've picked a hell of a time to tell me.'

Without warning, Gus's tight smile died. 'You sure you want to go through with this?' he asked quietly. 'This is dangerous shit, Rick.'

He could tell just how much Rick wanted to say, *Yeah, you're right. Let's call this whole thing off*, but to his credit his reply was only: 'How dangerous can it be, playing a dead man?'

★ ★ ★

In Speedbird's Kennedy Airport offices, president and CEO Warren Hicks looked soberly at the two Concorde crews in front of him and said: 'So there it is. These terrorists want the SST, and they need someone to fly it. Any volunteers?'

'I can't speak for the others,' said Captain Steven Whitmore, 'but I'll go.'

The second pilot — Renee Forester — immediately shook her head. 'You've got a family, Steve,' she said. 'I'll do it.'

'No way — '

'It's not even up for discussion,' she broke in sharply. 'You've got a wife and kids. Me . . . ' Her face shadowed for a moment. Then: 'Me . . . I'm a free agent.'

'Well, where *you* go, *I* go, boss,' said Mark Turner. His tone was light, but his dark eyes told a much different story.

'No,' she repeated.

'It's like you said,' he replied, joining her. 'It's not even up for discussion.'

'Anyone else want to be a hero?' asked Hicks.

Silence filled the room, save for an awkward shuffling of feet.

'Then I guess that's it,' he said heavily.

'All right,' said Gus. 'They're sending a tanker to refuel the Concorde and we've just got word that a pilot and crew are on the way with orders to take you wherever you want to go. We're doing everything you've asked for, okay? Just don't spook and do anything to harm Kimani.'

The line crackled for a moment. Then Aldo said: 'What about the Master?'

Gus hesitated. 'I need more time to get Shaguma here.'

'Forget it. An hour's all you've got!'

Inside the hangar, Aldo hung up. Through the window he and Cotton watched a tanker truck approach, then pass through the cordon of police cars. Its crew set to work refueling the SST. It took less time than they would have thought — about fifteen minutes. As soon as the tanker truck drove off, a tractor pulled a portable boarding ramp up to the aircraft's entry door. The ground-crew wheeled it into place and then disappeared into the aircraft so they could lock it down.

Hunched together in the cramped space between the side panels of the ramp were four ESU personnel known collectively for the purposes of this operation as Squad Two. Each man was heavily armed and armored, and each wore a miniaturized headset beneath his helmet.

As the ground-crew climbed back into the tractor and drove away, Gus said softly: 'They've got to walk Kimani from the hangar to the plane. That gives us about a hundred feet to nail them. Can you drop them all at once?'

Alessandro nodded. 'No problem. I've got three snipers on each cultist. You give the signal, they're dead.'

The radio squawked again. Gus snatched it up. Aldo said: 'We're coming out now. Don't you spook, got it?'

'Got it.'

All eyes focused on the hangar entrance. From this distance it was little more than a square, black shadow. For half a minute — the longest half-minute of Gus's life — nothing happened. Then he shifted fractionally. There was movement back there in the darkness.

The terrorists were coming out.

Beside him, Alessandro said: 'What the fuck — ?'

Gus's face tightened.

The terrorists were coming out of the hangar in single file — under cover of a long tarpaulin. It covered them so that they looked like some kind of headless Chinese New Year dragon, and made it impossible for the ESU snipers to select any one target and be sure it wasn't Secretary-General Kimani.

'The bastards!' breathed Alessandro. And then, into his ear-mike: 'All units — hold your fire! Repeat — *hold your fire!*'

The terrorists shuffled slowly toward the ramp. In the well behind the side boards, the four-man ESU team waited tensely, weapons ready, as they heard the cultists begin to climb the stairs. The curious procession slowly vanished inside the airplane. A moment later the door closed.

As they shrugged off the tarp, Aldo stabbed a finger at one of the cultists bringing up the rear and said: 'Get down

184

in the baggage bay! Shoot anyone who tries to break in!'

★ ★ ★

Outside, an ambulance crossed the field and drew to a halt beside Alessandro's REP. The rear doors opened and two more ESU officers posing as medics stepped out. One handed Gus a doctor's coat. He slipped it on and added a pair of glasses for good measure.

The agents lifted out the gurney upon which Rick was posing as Shaguma. Gus looked at him and felt yet another stir of misgivings. In the bright light of day it was anyone's guess whether or not he would fool Shaguma's disciples. But it was too late to back out now, even if they'd had the option.

'How you feeling, pal?' he asked quietly.

'Hopefully better than I look,' said Rick, his voice muffled by the bandages. He tipped his head forward a little to get a better look at Gus. 'That's *your* disguise?' he asked. 'For your sake, I sure hope they're near-sighted.'

'All I need is a few seconds.'

'Trust me, that's all you're gonna get.'

Another REP crossed the runway, headed toward them. It pulled up alongside the ambulance and Mark Turner climbed out, followed by —

Gus felt his stomach lurch and he shook his head.

'No fucking way!' he snapped. 'Get back in the car and get the hell out of here!'

Renee held her ground. 'Good to see you, too.'

'I'm not kidding, Renee!'

'Neither am I. This is what I do, remember?'

'I don't care! No! I'm in charge here, and you're not going!'

'It's me or nobody.'

'Then it's nobody.'

She tilted her head at him. 'Gus,' she said. 'Are you *pouting?*'

He turned away from her and slammed a fist into the side of the ambulance. With a show of bravado she really didn't feel inside, Renee turned to Alessandro and the others and said: 'He'll be fine in just a minute.'

★　★　★

'They're coming!' said Jasmine.

The cultists peered anxiously through the windows as two medics carried a gurney toward the plane. A doctor in glasses was walking beside the patient. Behind them came the pilots, one of them a woman.

Leaning across Kimani to get a look for himself, Cotton recognized Gus and Renee immediately, and allowed himself a smirk.

Aldo said: 'Open the door.'

Jasmine hurried to do as he said.

Just before they reached the ramp, Aldo called down: 'Stop! I want the pilot and co-pilot up here first!'

Gus and Renee exchanged a look. With his eyes he told her to go ahead. Renee and Mark started up the stairs. As soon as they stepped through the door, they were covered. Cotton came forward to pat Renee down. Aldo searched Mark.

Cotton's hand stopped between Renee's

legs and he groped her. She showed no reaction, but it was difficult. Cotton grinned and grabbed her butt.

'Enjoying yourself?' she asked at last.

Cotton nodded. 'Sure. You've got a great ass.'

He waited for Aldo to finish searching the co-pilot, then he shoved them both forward, toward the cramped cockpit. Aldo went back to the door and told Gus and the others to come ahead.

★ ★ ★

The radio in Alessandro's REP squawked and he grabbed it. 'Alessandro here,' he snapped. 'Talk.'

'Collins, Airport Security,' came the reply. 'I've got someone from SENTI-NEL on the line. They want to talk to Novacek.'

'Put 'em through,' said Alessandro, and a moment later: 'This is Lieutenant Alessandro, NYPD ESU. Novacek's not here right now.'

'Damn,' said the voice at the other end. 'Tell him we've just got an ID on a Jane

Doe who died at Coney Island Hospital last night. She was a member of Armageddon. We've ID'd the man who fetched her in, claiming she was his girlfriend. He's Armageddon, too, a man named Paige Cotton. Depending on what he saw or what he heard, it's just possible the sonofabitch already knows that Shaguma's dead.'

Alessandro felt his jaw slacken. 'Shit! If that's the case, Novacek could be walking into a trap.'

He watched Gus and the fake medics carry their equally fake Shaguma into the SST. As the door closed behind them he made a snap decision and said into his ear-mike: 'Squad Two! Get out of that ramp and prepare to board the aircraft!'

★ ★ ★

The side panels on the ramp swung open and the men of Squad Two made smoothly for the underbelly of the Concorde. The first one to reach the baggage hatch stuck a T-bar key into the

189

lock and prepared to open the door. The rest of the team congregated around him, weapons at the ready.

★ ★ ★

The Senitel agents carried the gurney into the plane. Gus followed them in and broke stride when he spotted Joseph Kimani seated about halfway down the plane. One of the cultists sat beside him, a handgun pressed into the Secretary-General's ribs. Then Aldo confronted them, his own hand wrapped around a Colt semi.

'Hold it,' he said.

They obeyed.

He searched Gus and the medics for weapons while Jasmine came forward and ran a gentle palm across the blanket covering the man she believed to be Shaguma, searching for any weapons they might have hidden there. The cultist keeping an eye on Renee and Mark chanced a look over his shoulder, anxious to see for himself the condition of their beloved master. As he did so, Mark slowly reached down and unhooked the gun from beneath his seat, where the ground-crew had stowed it earlier.

Renee glared at him and shook her head.

He gave her a slight, helpless shrug that said: *We've got to do something.*

At last Aldo gestured to the man on the gurney and said: 'Take him down to the end of the plane.'

Cotton had been lounging in a seat at the back of the aircraft. He watched the medics lower the legs of the gurney and then wheel Shaguma along the narrow aisle toward him. When Gus made to follow them, however, Aldo shook his head. 'You stay here,' he said.

Gus fixed him with a stern look. 'If you want that man to stay alive, he needs *this*.' He held up the bag of plasma he was carrying. 'Are you qualified to give it to him?'

Aldo mulled it over for a moment before stepping aside.

Gus followed the medics along the narrow aisle. As he closed on Kimani, he locked gazes with the man. He didn't know if the Secretary-General read the truth in his eyes. He hoped so. Kimani would have to act quickly once the shit hit the fan.

At that moment Cotton got up, Uzi still in hand, and shot the two medics.

Then he shot Rick.

Gus froze, thinking: *Oh my god, my god, no* —

Startled by the shooting, the cultist who'd been charged with guarding Kimani turned to see what was going on. Kimani immediately saw the chance he'd been waiting for, and grabbed the girl by the wrist.

Gus threw himself down, pulled a gun from where it had been secreted under the gurney and shot the girl, then threw himself at Kimani and pushed him down between the seats.

In the cockpit, Mark turned in the co-pilot's seat and shot the cultist who'd been watching them. The bullet hit the man in the stomach, punched him up against the wall. He collapsed in a heap.

★   ★   ★

Beneath the plane, the leading Squad Two man twisted the T-bar key in the lock, tore open the door and reached inside for the pull-down ladder. As the hatch opened, the cultist Aldo had dispatched to keep an eye on things there fired his Uzi and killed three of the four officers in his first burst. A second later the cultist broke cover and came after them, shooting and wounding the fourth man. As the wounded man fell, his finger tightened reflexively on the trigger of his H&K MP5. Bullets sprayed across the wing surface.

Jet fuel immediately started dripping from the holes.

A moment later the cultist stuck his head through the hatch, saw the lone survivor and emptied the Uzi at him. The ESU man saw him at the same moment and opened fire. Each man killed the other in the blink of an eye.

13

Alessandro yelled: 'Squad Three, Squad Three — move in! Move in!'

Inside the plane, Gus was still exchanging gunfire with the remaining cultists from behind one of the seats. He was outnumbered and it was only a matter of seconds before they decided to rush him. Somewhere behind him he heard Renee scream, *'No!'* and a moment later Mark came out of the cockpit to give him a hand. Cotton shot him in the right leg and Mark buckled and went down.

Outside, the six men of Squad Three thundered up the ramp and started struggling with the locked door, and in that moment there was an almost shockingly abrupt lull in the gunfire. Everyone left alive kept their heads down, deafened by the confined gunshots. Kimani opened his mouth to say something. Gus silenced him with a shake of the head.

It was then that he heard an ominous *clink*.

He looked down and saw a pin lying in the aisle next to him.

A *grenade* pin.

Ducked behind a seat toward the back of the plane, Cotton held up the grenade to which it belonged. His thumb held down the pin-less trigger lever.

'Hey, Novacek!'

Gus hesitated, then looked around the seat, not over it.

'Here's your choice,' called Cotton. 'Hand me back the pin, or I lob this sucker right into your laps.'

Gus swore silently.

'You know I'm not fucking around,' said Cotton.

Outside, the ESU team's attempts to open the locked door were temporarily suspended as they tried to work out the reason for the sudden silence. Gus looked back down the aisle at Mark, slumped in the cockpit door, and beyond him Renee, looking back at him. It wasn't such a hard decision after all, he thought. If he refused to play ball, they'd die here, all of them, just the way Rick and the other two SENTINEL agents had died. While they lived Gus still had a chance to turn this around.

He threw down his gun, picked up the pin and then helped Kimani to his feet.

Four cultists were still alive — Cotton, Aldo, Jasmine and a tall, skinny Cuban with a long neck and a bald head, whose name was Elian. Jasmine went directly to the body on the gurney and started weeping. Cotton took the pin from Gus, stuck it back in the grenade, then thumbed speed-dial on the cell phone in his other hand and thrust it at him.

'Tell your men outside to back off.'

Gus took the phone, cleared his throat, said: 'Collins? This is Novacek.'

'Novacek! Did you get 'em? What about Kimani — ?'

'They're still calling the shots, Collins, but Kimani's right beside me and he's unharmed. Tell Alessandro to pull his men back. Got it?'

Collins was silent for a moment. Then he said softly: 'Is this a bluff?'

'No. Do it.'

Cotton peered through one of the windows. Twenty seconds passed. Then he saw the ESU team outside begin to withdraw. Satisfied, he turned back to the others and focused on Jasmine.

'Don't waste your fuckin' tears on *that*,' he said, pointing to the blood-spattered gurney. 'Whoever it was, he wasn't the Master.'

He felt Aldo watching him, suspicious. 'How did you know?'

'Ask Novacek.'

Aldo pointed his Uzi at Gus. 'Where's His Holiness?'

Gus looked at the body on the gurney, the dark bloodstain spreading across the blanket, and he thought about the man beneath it, the friend he'd involved in this and gotten killed. 'Shaguma died in hospital on Friday night,' he said softly. Then he looked directly at Cotton. 'You were there. I guess you forgot to tell them, huh?'

Aldo scowled. 'You want to tell me what the fuck's going on?'

'Sure,' said Cotton.

Then he brought the Uzi up and blew a

hole through Aldo's stomach.

Jasmine screamed. Aldo stumbled back, came up hard against one of the seats and collapsed in the aisle.

As Elian started to bring up his own weapon, Cotton covered him and snapped: 'You want to die, too?'

Jasmine answered for both of them. 'We're all willing to die.'

'For what?' demanded Cotton. 'Armageddon's dead. I'm offering you a chance to live.' He looked at Gus. 'New plan, Novacek. Kimani for ten million dollars.'

Jasmine frowned. 'What're you doing?'

'I'll give you half,' said Cotton. 'That's two and a half million each — and that buys a lot of resurrection.'

Jasmine sneered at him. 'You're nothing but a criminal.'

'You just figured that out?'

'Aren't you forgetting Alex?' asked Gus.

Cotton's cheek twitched at the sound of his son's name. 'That's not my call anymore,' he said flatly. 'I've done all I can for him. Now I gotta get on with my own life.'

'At your son's expense?'

'You won't hurt him. That would make you just like me. And you don't have the balls to be me. That's why I'll always beat you.' He gestured to the phone Gus still held in his hand. 'Now, make the fuckin' call.'

Gus hesitated, something inside him still wrenched askew by Rick's murder. Then he sighed and punched in a very special number. A moment later he said: 'Mr. President? It's Novacek. Secretary Kimani is alive and unhurt, but they want ten million dollars or they'll kill him.'

He listened to the silence at the other end of the line. He could imagine the President at his desk, staring at the speakerphone, and seated on the couches in front of him the directors of the CIA, the FBI, the NSA and their various advisors.

'Just a minute, Gus,' said the President. He looked up, his expression asking the question.

One of his advisors nodded. 'We can get the money, no problem.'

'How long?'

'An hour. Maybe less.'

'Did you hear that, Novacek?' asked the President.

'Yes, sir,' said Gus. To Cotton he said: 'The money's coming. One million now, nine million when you hand over Kimani.'

Cotton showed him a mirthless grin. 'Jesus Christ! Do I look that stupid to you?'

In his ear, Gus heard the President say: 'Novacek? What're you doing?'

Gus took the phone away from his ear and ended the call. 'Then you'd better pull the pin,' he said. 'I'm sorry, Mr. Secretary.'

Ever the statesman, Kimani said only: 'I understand.'

Gus watched Cotton closely, wondering if this was a bluff too far. Cotton looked just crazy enough to pull the pin and send them all to hell to prove a point. But then some of the tension drained out of him.

'You're a hell of a poker player, Novacek. When am I gonna get my other nine million?'

'Give me the name of the country that accepts garbage like you and I'll have the money transferred to a bank there.'

Cotton weighed that and then nodded. 'Dump the bodies,' he told Jasmine and Elian. Then to Kimani: 'I bet you wish you'd never come to New York, huh, Mr. Secretary?'

* * *

While Jasmine and Elian cleared the plane, wordlessly carrying the bodies down to the baggage hold and dropping them through the open hatch onto the runway below, Renee grabbed the emergency first aid kit and did what she could to stop the flow of blood from Mark Turner's leg wound. Cotton shoved Kimani into a seat and said: 'Mr. Novacek and I are going up front. You make one move I don't like and I'll gut-shoot Novacek and let him die real slow.'

Kimani matched his gaze. 'I'm not going anywhere,' he said almost gently.

Cotton pushed Gus ahead of him until

they reached Renee. Gus looked down at her as she finished working on Mark. When she returned his gaze her face was pale and tight. But there was an entire book to be read in her eyes, and it wrenched at him still further because it was a love story about a love that would now never come to anything.

'You okay?' he asked.

Her smile was brief, quirky and entirely humorless. 'That's a pretty dumb question.'

'I'm a pretty dumb guy,' he said. 'I must be, the way I treated you.'

'Oh, puh-*lease*,' said Cotton, grinning again.

Between them, Gus and Renee made Mark as comfortable as possible and then went through to the cramped, instrument-filled cockpit, where Cotton gestured that Gus should take the co-pilot's seat. A heavy silence settled then, until about an hour later the radio suddenly came to life.

'Speedbird Five, do you read me? Come in, Speedbird Five.'

Renee looked at Cotton, who nodded.

She answered the call. 'This is Speedbird Five. Over.'

'Speedbird Five, this is Agent John Daniels of the FBI. I have the money and I'll be there in three minutes. Copy that?'

'I copy,' said Renee.

Cotton shifted his weight a little in anticipation. 'Awright!' he said. 'Fire this puppy up, baby. We're getting *out* of here.'

As Renee got busy at the controls and the Concorde's Rolls-Royce Olympus turbojet engines came to life, Cotton ambled back down toward Kimani. He flopped into the seat beside him and said: 'You know somethin'? I could never have pulled this off without your help.'

'What did I do?' asked Kimani.

'Back in London, you stopped your motorcade to take flowers from a little girl in a wheelchair, remember? That's when it hit me. You're a sucker for kids.'

'It's unfortunate that you turned an act of kindness into something evil.'

'What can I tell you? No good deed goes unpunished.'

'Cotton!'

Cotton came up out of his seat. Gus was standing in the cockpit doorway. He hooked a thumb over his shoulder. 'The money's here,' he said.

Cotton hurried forward again, stared out through the tinted windshield just as a helicopter settled on the tarmac in front of them. As the rotors slowed, the passenger-side door opened and a dark-haired man in a pale gray suit jumped out, carrying a metal briefcase. He hurried out from under the downdraft and then disappeared around the side of the aircraft. A few moments later they heard him bang on the door.

Cotton called out: 'Elian! Open the door and take the case. Don't expose yourself any more than you have to, and don't let that agent start a conversation with you!'

Elian nodded and went to do as he'd been told. He opened the door, took the case, closed and locked the door again. A few moments later the FBI agent came back into view through the windshield. He walked backward, away from the plane, turned and climbed back into the chopper. The rotors started turning faster again, and then the chopper lifted off the ground and headed back the way it had come.

Cotton hurried back through the aircraft and told Elian to set the case down and check it over for booby-traps. Elian worked quickly and thoroughly. At last Cotton gave the order for the case to be opened. Elian worked the catches, still half-expecting the case to explode with tear gas or some other debilitating nerve agent. Nothing happened. He pushed the lid back to reveal neatly-wrapped stacks of dollar bills in various denominations — a million dollars in all.

Cotton looked down the aisle at Jasmine. 'Tell the truth, now,' he grinned. 'Ain't this better than dying for a cause?'

She gave him a withering look and turned away.

'Somehow, I don't think she feels the money's as important as you do.'

Cotton whirled back toward Gus. 'She also thought Shaguma was god.' He turned his attention to Renee. 'Okay — get us out of here, baby.'

Renee held his gaze for a moment, then faced front again. She flipped some switches, and the nose-cone slowly lowered. 'This is Speedbird Five, Kennedy Tower. Clear to taxi.'

'Speedbird Five, this is Kennedy Tower. Proceed to runway four-six. All other traffic has been diverted to allow you immediate take-off. Wind zero ninety knots. Good luck to you.'

'Speedbird Five taking off runway four-six.' She looked around again. 'Better strap yourself in, Cotton, and tell your people to do likewise.'

As she faced front she saw Gus looking at her. He said: 'What do you want me to do?'

She considered the question briefly. 'I've got no co-pilot and no navigator. I'm scared shitless and I can hardly think straight. I think prayer might be a good place to start, don't you?'

Then she was all business again, and as she pushed the accelerators forward a tremor ran through the jet aircraft and it started to inch forward.

'Up to one hundred . . . one-fifty . . . '

The plane thundered along the runway, accelerating steadily. There was some more minor turbulence. Gus took his eyes off the blurring tarmac ahead and studied Renee's profile. She was wholly focused on the job at hand. Then she began to ease back on the yoke and the runway dropped away beneath them. As the plane speared skyward, she pointed at two rows of switches and said: 'Flip those up.'

He did so, and the wing-flaps and landing-gear retracted.

They were on their way.

Part Four

The Atlantic

14

In the Oval Office, the President and his advisors gathered around a floor-to-ceiling map of the world. A small, pulsing circle of light showed the direction of the plane as it flew out over the Atlantic.

'What have we got deployed out there?' asked the President.

Admiral George Moore Jnr., the Chief of Naval Operations, said: 'The *Kitty Hawk*'s on her way to the Med.'

'That's Joe Gunn's ship, right?'

'Yes, Mr. President. Good man.'

'All right. Contact him, Admiral. Tell him what's going on and have him ready to scramble fighters at my orders.'

★   ★   ★

With his blue eyes fixed on the rolling gray sea rising and falling beyond the safety glass, Captain Joseph P. Gunn said into the phone: 'Tell the President they'll be ready to launch whenever he gives the word.' He hung up and turned to his executive officer. 'Bring up two Tomcats and put them on red alert. I'll be in C.D.C.'

'Aye, Captain!'

While Gunn made his way down to the Combat Detection Center, two F-14s were rolled onto elevators and lifted to the flight deck. As deck personnel — nicknamed *shooters* — readied them for take-off, four crewmen, a pilot and navigator for each machine, ran across the carrier's non-slip deck toward them.

As soon as Gunn closed the C.D.C. door behind him, one of the technicians turned away from his screen and reported: 'Here's your SST, Captain.'

Gunn studied the green blip that pulsed brighter with every passing sweep of the ship's radar. 'I want tracking reports every five minutes. Any change of course, notify me immediately.'

'Aye, aye, sir.'

★ ★ ★

Renee swallowed hard and forced herself to relax as much as possible. So far, so good. They were airborne, they were heading out over the sea, and they were still in one piece. But there was still one particular piece of information Cotton hadn't yet seen fit to share with them.

'I need to know our destination,' she said without turning around.

'Algiers,' Cotton said from the narrow doorway.

She shook her head. 'We can't land there. The runways are too short.'

'Not too short,' Cotton replied. 'Just shorter than recommended by safety regulations.'

'Either way, it's a hell of a risk when you've got nine million dollars waiting for you,' said Gus.

Cotton seemed unconcerned. 'No risk, no gain, I always say.'

'That explains why you snatched Kimani when you didn't have to.'

Cotton eyed him curiously, his silence inviting Gus to go on.

'We'd have paid you as much just for giving up Shaguma,' Gus said. 'You could

213

be sitting on a beach somewhere by now, instead of heading for some shithole in Algeria.'

'I don't know what the fuck you're talking about.'

'Why don't I believe that?'

Cotton stepped around the empty navigator's seat and pressed his gun against Gus's head, suddenly white with rage. 'Why don't I just kill you right now, Novacek?'

'Because you want the money.'

'Keep fuckin' with me, man, and money or no money, I'll blow your head off.'

He turned and stormed out. Gus watched him go, then realized Renee was looking at him.

'Do you have a death wish?' she asked.

Jasmine, taking Cotton's place in the doorway, said: 'What did you mean just now? About 'giving up' the Master?'

He eyed her for a long moment. 'Who do you think gave us the location of the safe-house?' he asked at length.

'Cotton? Never!'

'Think about it. He's the only one who

was in this for the money.'

'And he sold the Master out?'

'What can I tell you? I guess acolytes ain't what they used to be.'

* * *

Captain Gunn was back on deck when he got the first report from the C.D.C.

'Captain, the SST is headed in our direction. Eighty thousand feet. Air speed: 1600 knots. Course: 145 due east.'

'Roger that, C.D.C.' The executive officer handed him a red phone. Gunn said: 'Mr. President . . . ?'

'Just hold on a moment, Captain.'

Back in the Oval Office, someone — to Gunn it sounded like Admiral Moore — said: 'Launch a couple of chase planes, sir. Show them we mean business.'

Another voice said: 'That's just going to escalate the situation, sir.'

'Well, we can't just sit here and do nothing,' argued Moore. 'The whole world's watching us.'

'What do we gain by having planes up there?' asked the President. 'They know we're not going to shoot down the Secretary-General.'

The Admiral said: 'What if they fly below radar and we lose them?'

Silence, as the President considered his options. And then: 'Captain Gunn — launch two chase planes. But have them stay out of visual range of the SST for now.'

'Yes, sir,' said Gunn.

Thirty seconds later the two F-14s were launched.

* * *

Troubled as much by what she'd seen as what she'd heard, Jasmine went in search of Elian and found him keeping watch on Mark. In whispers she told him what Gus had told her about Cotton.

'Why would Cotton tip off SENTINEL?' Elian asked when she was finished.

'To get rid of His Holiness and get us to kidnap Kimani,' she replied. 'This is all about money.'

Elian's expression hardened, because Jasmine had only confirmed his own growing suspicions. 'Then let's kill the sonofabitch and take this plane out,' he grated.

'We can do that,' she agreed. 'But if we live, we can keep Armageddon alive. What's more important?'

She broke off quickly as Cotton came along the aisle. 'I told you to keep watch on the cockpit,' he barked. 'Get your ass back there!'

She exchanged a final look with Elian and moved off.

* * *

In the cockpit, Renee said: 'That's odd.'

Gus took his eyes off the endless expanse of sky and ocean in front of them. 'What's wrong?'

Renee gestured to the fuel gauges. 'We're leaking fuel. We must be.'

'How long have we got?'

'Thirty minutes. Maybe less.'

'Great.'

He got up and left the cockpit, keeping his hands high so as not to spook Jasmine into doing anything foolish. She barred his way, but he could see that her heart was no longer in it. 'Let me pass,' he said. 'There's something Cotton needs to know.'

She hesitated and then stepped aside. 'No tricks,' she warned.

'No tricks.'

She kept him covered all the way down to where Cotton and Kimani were seated. Cotton stiffened when he saw Gus coming, and jumped to his feet. 'Where do you think you're going?'

Gus ignored him, sidestepped toward a window that overlooked the starboard delta-shaped wing and then swore. 'We've got a problem, Cotton.'

Cotton came closer, expecting some kind of trick, but grudgingly followed Gus's line of sight. He too saw the bullet holes stitched across the plane's carbon-composite wing, the fuel spilling from them in silver-yellow streams.

'We've got about thirty minutes' flying-time left, tops,' said Gus. 'We've got to turn back.'

Cotton curled his lip at that. 'Turn *back*? Are you fuckin' crazy?'

'*You* are, if you think there's enough fuel left to get us anywhere else.'

Stubbornly Cotton shook his head and indicated that Gus should head back to the cockpit. He went, with Cotton shadowing him every step of the way. 'You must think I'm fuckin' stupid. Man, I used that 'we're out of gas' routine back in high school.'

'So check the gauges for yourself.'

'I intend to.'

A moment later the plane gave an unpleasant lurch that almost threw them off their feet. As Renee leveled them up again, Elian jabbed a finger out the window. Cotton stepped back, away from Gus, took another look at the starboard wing. A chunk of metal had peeled back from one of the bullet holes.

He looked back at Gus, said: 'Go.'

In the cockpit, a warning buzzer had started to sound, and red lights were blinking frantically above the flaps switches, indicating — as if they needed telling — that the flaps had started to malfunction.

'We're losing altitude,' Renee reported as they joined her. 'I'm taking her down low and cutting our speed to conserve fuel. It's a Band-Aid at best, but we're not exactly full of choices.'

She eased the stick forward and the SST began a steady dive toward the waiting ocean.

'Okay,' said Cotton. 'So what are our options?'

'Besides *crash* and *drown*, you mean?'

'Don't get smart with me now . . . *Renee.*'

Gus dropped back into the co-pilot's seat and reached for the headset. 'I'll contact the White House, see if there are any ships nearby.'

'What'll that buy us?'

'Our lives, if we're lucky. Unless, of course, you're really anxious to find out what the bottom of the ocean looks like?'

Cotton's teeth clenched. 'Make the damn' call,' he spat.

'Mr. President . . . do you read me?'

There was a crackle of static. The plane gave another lurch. Renee leveled them out again. 'Mr. President?'

And then:

'Go ahead, Gus.'

220

'Sir, we're almost out of fuel and I think we're going to have to ditch. Are there any ships in our vicinity that might pick us up?'

'The *Kitty Hawk*. It's about two hundred miles from you.'

Gus looked at Renee, who could hear the exchange through her own headset. She nodded. 'I think we can make that.'

'I'll notify the captain,' said the President.

Gus frowned suddenly. 'The *Kitty Hawk*, Mr. President? Hold on, sir.' To Renee he said: 'Can you land this baby on a carrier?'

She opened her mouth to say one thing and instead said another. 'Oh, sure. With my eyes closed.'

'*Can* you?' he persisted.

'Don't be ridiculous. I'd have a better shot at landing on the moon.'

But Gus refused to give up on the idea. 'Mr. President, we'd like to try to land on the carrier.'

'*What?*'

Ignoring Renee's outburst he said: 'Will you clear it for us, sir?'

'Hold on, Gus.'

In the Oval Office, the President looked at Admiral Moore. Moore said: 'It can't be done, sir. Largest plane ever to land on a flat-top was a four-engine G-130 — and it crashed.'

'Want to tell that to the Press?' asked the President. When no one in the room responded, he said into the phone: 'Gus, I'll talk to the captain, have him contact you.'

'We'll be waiting, sir. We're not going anywhere . . . yet.'

*   *   *

The President called Gunn right away. 'I've already been told it can't be done, Captain. Now I'd like to hear how you're going to do it.'

'I'll talk to damage control, sir,' said Gunn. 'See what they can rig up.'

Gunn swapped the red phone for a black one. 'Bridge, this is the captain. We've got an uninvited bird landing . . .'

' 'Uninvited', sir?' asked the first officer

at the other end of the line.

'You heard me. Head us into the wind and tell the engine room to give me everything they've got.'

'Aye, aye, sir.'

* * *

Renee kept the SST as steady as possible, but it was getting increasingly difficult. The sea was no more than a hundred feet below them — far too close for comfort. She checked the screen that computed airspeed against fuel/mileage and said: 'At this speed and altitude, we've got about fifteen minutes before we go down.'

Cotton pulled out his grenade and toyed with it. 'Maybe we'd all be better off if I blew us up right now.'

Gus couldn't tell whether or not he really meant it. 'Mean you'd give up the other nine million that easily?'

'If we land on that fuckin' carrier, I'm kissing it goodbye anyway.'

'Forget the carrier!' said Renee. 'I told you I can't — '

'Why'd you have to lose the money?' asked Gus. 'You'd still have Kimani to bargain with. You could — '

Without warning, the radio came to life. 'Speedbird Five, Speedbird Five, this is Captain Joseph Gunn of the USS *Kitty Hawk*. Do you read me? Over.'

Renee said: 'Go ahead, Captain.'

'I've been instructed to help you land on our deck. Here are our coordinates . . . longitude 21 degrees . . . latitude 23.'

'Longitude two-one degrees, latitude two-three degrees. Roger that, Captain.'

'I've got two chase planes headed your way. Expect to see them any second. They'll help guide you in.'

'I see 'em,' said Gus.

'Captain, we have a visual on those aircraft.'

The two F-14s appeared as black dots against the cloudless sky, then grew rapidly in size until they flew right overhead, banked and then came back, one matching the Concorde's speed on either flank.

'What's your air speed, Five?'

'Three hundred knots. I'll drop it to 190 when I'm in sight of the carrier, but anything lower than that and I'll be dangerously close to stalling out.'

Gunn was silent for a moment. Finally he said: 'That's about fifty knots faster than our birds land, but we'll do everything in our power to stop you. Oh, and be prepared for your landing gear to collapse — '

'My landing gear?'

'I doubt if it's built to withstand this kind of impact.'

'Wonderful.'

'Damage control is rigging extra crash nets on the flight deck. Hopefully, they'll do the trick.' He paused briefly before adding: 'I, ah, don't suppose you've had any experience landing on flat-tops, have you?'

'I've never even flown *over* an aircraft carrier, Captain, much less *onto* one.'

'Well, there's always a first time, Captain Forester.'

Gus shook his head. 'Why don't you tell him about the wing-flaps, so he can have a *real* laugh?'

Gunn said: 'We're going to do everything we can to bring you in safe and sound, Speedbird Five.'

'I'm holding you to that, Captain,' said Renee. 'Out.'

15

Cotton went back along the aisle, pillows and blankets in hand. When he reached Kimani he dropped the pillows into his lap. 'We're going to be landing on an aircraft carrier,' he said.

Kimani frowned briefly. 'Is that possible?'

'We'll soon find out.'

'Maybe a prayer wouldn't hurt.'

'Why not? Knock yourself out.'

Kimani closed his eyes for a long moment. Cotton watched him, curious. 'Scared of dying, Mr. Secretary?' he asked with a smirk.

The statesman opened his eyes again. 'I'm prepared for it,' he replied.

Cotton chuckled. 'Come on. You're as scared as the rest of them, aren't you?'

'What is there to fear about dying?'

'Well, for one thing, you can't come back if you don't like it.'

Kimani smiled. 'I wasn't joking just

now. I *am* prepared. I've led a good life, I've tried to do right by my family, my people, and by the people of the world, and I think I've made a good job of it. My only regret is that I couldn't do more. But what about you? If there *is* an Afterlife, and you are called to account, how will *you* fare, Mr. Cotton? Are *you* prepared?'

The corners of Cotton's eyes and mouth tightened dangerously. He pointed to the pillows and blankets and said: 'Take those and get to the back of the plane, then pad yourself well. You're worth a lot of money to me — and no matter how this comes out, it ain't going to be pleasant.'

* * *

Gus flipped the switches Renee told him to flip, but the flaps remained locked where they were.

'Keep trying,' she said. 'Somehow we've got to get those flaps working.'

'I'm trying, believe me, but they've jammed solid.'

'Well, what was already futile just

became impossible.'

Gus shook his head. 'A wise man once said: Failure is not the missing of success, but the giving up of trying.'

She looked at him and made an incredulous kind of chuffing sound. 'That's it?' she said. 'That's your pearl of wisdom for today?' She almost laughed, but couldn't quite make it. 'You *do* realize that without flaps we've lost even the remotest chance of landing safely.'

'Of course I do. But at the risk of sounding like a very bad novel, I can't think of anyone else I'd sooner have in my corner right now than you.'

Renee said: 'Gus, this is neither the time nor the place for — '

'It's *exactly* the time and the place,' he said. 'I goofed up, Ren. I was so busy getting caught up in my own feelings that I forgot to consider yours, and I'm sorry, more sorry than you'll ever know. But that's not to say I ever forgot what a lucky man I was, or how much I did — *do* — love you.'

She looked at him through liquid eyes. She wanted to speak but words failed her.

At last she squared her shoulders, sniffed, and said: 'Okay. You've had your say. Now I'll have mine.' And she put her green eyes back on the windshield ahead and said: 'Let's get this motherfucker down in one piece.'

* * *

Aboard the *Kitty Hawk*, preparations were already well advanced for the landing. No one believed it was really possible. No one saw any reason to think that what happened today would change that view. But this wasn't about landing. This was, as Captain Gunn had said, all about damage control.

Air-sea rescue choppers took off, preparing to take up station around the carrier and go into action the minute the SST ditched. The deck was cleared of aircraft. Fire trucks stood ready in front of the vast control tower amidships, their crews tense and silent as they scanned the sky for their first sight of the incoming bird.

Marked by their distinctive yellow

jumpsuits, damage-control crews were everywhere. Some raised the crash net at the end of the deck. Others quickly rigged four more crash nets between the cross-deck pendants and six-foot tow-bars, each one at twenty-foot intervals. These wouldn't contain the Concorde, but they might at least slow its landing speed sufficiently to stop it crashing right off the far edge.

Still more deck-crews lined up all the so-called 'yellow equipment' — tractors, loaders, forklifts — along the opposite edge of the carrier to form a barricade to stop the SST from sliding off into the water. Three Jet Blast Deflectors — the huge, angled steel plates that absorb the jet blast as planes take off — were raised hydraulically at the front of the takeoff runway in case the SST veered off course.

A yellow crane weighing almost seventy tons was positioned about a hundred feet from the far end of the flight deck to stop the SST if it broke through all the deck cables and crash nets.

Gunn watched all the activity from the bridge, taking his eyes off the deck only when his air boss, the officer in charge of landings, said: 'With all due respect to you and the President, sir, this is nuts.'

Gunn shrugged. 'Maybe it is, at that,' he agreed. 'But I promised those poor bastards we'd do everything we could for them, and as far as I'm concerned that's exactly what we're gonna do.'

★　★　★

Renee looked down at the fuel gauge indicator. It was bumping on empty. She said: 'Remember that Easter weekend we spent on the beach at Brighton?'

Gus glanced at her. 'When the water was so damn cold I wouldn't go in and you thought I couldn't swim?' He chuckled at the memory. 'What about it?'

'This water's going to be a *lot* colder.'

He smile died. 'Thanks for sharing that with me.'

Standing in the cockpit doorway, Jasmine listened to their conversation, reached a decision and turned away. She hurried along the aisle to Cotton, who looked up at her expectantly. She opened her mouth, as if to ask him a question — then slammed him on the temple with the butt of her Beretta. He slumped sideways, hurt but still conscious.

Before he could recover, Jasmine grabbed the grenade out of his jacket pocket, pulled the pin and showed it to him.

Cotton struggled to focus his glazed eyes on it.

'See this, motherfucker?' she asked through gritted teeth. 'We're all going to paradise!'

'F-For Chrissake, Jasmine!' he managed, 'give me that fuckin' pin!'

But Jasmine only backed up the aisle, fanatical rage twisting her features out of shape. 'Fuck you!'

'W-what about Armageddon?' he asked, blood trickling from the cut in his temple. 'Your five million?'

'It'll never happen,' Elian told him, coming to join her. 'And we want to make sure you die knowing it.'

Jasmine released the trigger and Cotton dove for cover, yelling: *'Shit!'*

A second later the grenade went off,

obliterating Jasmine and Elian and blowing a door-sized hole in the side of the plane, just above the starboard wing.

The F-14 pilot on that side of the plane flinched and quickly banked his machine wing-over, away from the sudden rush of debris. '*Kitty Hawk*, this is Red Dog One. An explosion just blew a hole in the SST's fuselage.'

Gunn came back at him even before he stopped talking. 'Are they going down?'

'Negative, sir. Not *yet*, anyway.'

* * *

The entire plane rocked and in the aftermath of the explosion various alarms started bleating. Renee, fighting to control the aircraft, yelled: 'What the hell blew up?'

Gus dragged himself out of his seat. 'I'll find out.'

The answer became obvious as soon as he entered the main cabin. There was no missing the gaping hole in the side of the plane, no ignoring the pummel and howl of the wind, the red and charred black smudge that was all that remained of Jasmine and Elian.

From the seat into which they'd helped him, Mark said: 'She blew them up. The g-girl, Jasmine, I mean. She got hold of a grenade and blew them up.'

Gus looked down at him. He looked pale and sweaty, pained and shocked. He nodded. Then, using the seat-backs, he hauled himself toward Kimani and helped the statesman to his feet. Eyes narrowed, hair flying everywhere, he bawled: 'Are you okay, Mr. Secretary?'

Kimani nodded, but he looked distinctly ashen, shocked more by what he'd seen Jasmine do than by the consequence of her action.

He moved on. Chunks of debris lay everywhere. The corpses of Jasmine and Elian lay between the damaged seats. And a few rows further back he saw Cotton, also sprawled between seats, blood splattered everywhere around him. He turned and dragged himself back to Kimani.

'Well, at least we don't have to worry about them anymore.'

Kimani only shrugged. 'No matter whose life it is, the loss is always tragic.'

Gus looked at the gaping hole and damaged wing beyond, thinking that Kimani had a bigger heart and a more forgiving nature than he ever would. Then all thought stopped as an idea occurred to him.

He hustled forward again.

As Renee fought to keep the SST in the air he leaned over and kissed her cheek. She shot him a look.

'More bad news?'

'*Au contraire, mon cheri.* This time I've got a great idea.'

'I don't want to hear it,' she said.

He told her anyway.

* ★ ★ ★

On the *Kitty Hawk's* flight deck, the Damage Control Chief said: 'We've done everything we can, sir, but the truth is without a tail-hook that aircraft hasn't a hope in hell of stopping.'

Captain Gunn took that in grim silence.

'There's still time to use foam, sir,' the Damage Control Chief added.

'No, I've made my decision about that,' said Gunn, 'and I'm sticking with it.'

'Aye, sir. And I don't mean to question your judgment, but if she burns . . . '

'Then you'll deal with it,' Gunn said firmly. 'We're gonna have enough trouble trying to stop this bird without turning the deck into a mud slide before it even gets here. Now, get your men to safety, chief. And if you know any prayers, say 'em.'

* * *

Kimani hauled himself up to the cockpit just in time to hear Renee say: 'That's the worst idea you've ever had in your entire life.'

'I knew you'd like it,' he said, and he grinned. He actually *grinned*.

'Why don't I just shoot you, instead?' she asked.

''Cause then we can't make love later.'

'You do this, you idiot, and there won't *be* any later.'

'Can you land this plane without the flaps working?' he demanded.

'I can't land this bloody plane even *with* the flaps working — uh, pardon my language, Mr. Secretary. I didn't see you standing there.'

Gus said: 'Try.'

He kissed her again, then turned to Kimani and said: 'If you'll come with me, Mr. Secretary . . . '

He led Kimani back into the crew area behind the cockpit and rummaged around in the emergency toolkit until he found two long screwdrivers, explaining the plan, such as it was, as he went. Kimani listened in silence until he was finished. Then he said: 'You *are* joking, of course?'

'I don't mean to be disrespectful, sir,' Gus replied, holding up the screwdrivers, 'but do I *look* like I'm joking?'

'No. That's what worries me.'

'Well, let's get to it. Mark? How do you feel?'

'Like I want to do something useful to take my mind of the pain.'

'I think we can arrange that,' said Gus.

238

Using knives from the galley cutlery drawer he and Kimani started cutting the seatbelts out of the chairs and passing them to Mark, who triple-knotted them all together. It was a crude attempt at best, but better than nothing. When Gus judged that they'd jury-rigged a lifeline that was long enough, he took one end and triple-knotted it around his waist. Using the chair-backs, he and Kimani then dragged themselves toward the hole in the starboard side. When he judged he was close enough, Gus stopped and studied the ragged-edged gash.

'Having second thoughts?' asked Kimani. 'No one would blame you if were.'

Gus only said: 'Make sure you get a firm grip on your end of this line.'

'I won't let you down.'

Gus picked a path over the debris and carefully crawled out onto the wide, exposed wing. The F-14 pilot a short distance away wondered what the hell he was doing. Gus wondered the same thing himself as he paused and lay flat, waiting for his heart to stop pounding. A gust of wind stronger than the rest almost blew him right toward the edge and into the sea. He glanced back over one shoulder. Kimani, clinging to the other end of the makeshift rope and making sure he was well braced to take Gus's weight, nodded. *It's all right, I've got you.* Gus nodded back and then went to work.

He stabbed the right-hand screwdriver into the wing, piercing the thin metal skin. Then, clinging to it, he reached ahead and stuck the left-hand screwdriver into the wing. Working slowly in this manner, he gradually pulled himself forward across the wing surface, toward the damaged flaps.

Progress was tortuously slow, but there was no way to rush it. The slipstream tore at his hair and clothes, forcing him to narrow his eyes to slits. He wrenched the left-hand screwdriver free, stretched ahead, rammed it back into the wing and dragged himself a little further forward.

Kimani, following his every move through worried eyes, heard someone praying in an undertone. He was surprised when he recognized his own voice.

The lifeline around Gus's waist went taut. For one brief moment he was afraid they hadn't made it long enough. Kimani edged a little closer to the hole and the makeshift rope slackened. Gus kept going.

At last he reached the damaged flaps. He clung to the wing surface, drenched in sweat, breathing hard. Then he let go of the embedded right-hand screwdriver and started to wrench the twisted metal back and forth to free it from the gap into which it had gotten wedged.

The point of the curled-under piece of metal was buried deep inside the mechanism that controlled the raising and lowering of the flaps. He shifted position a little, trying to ignore the white-capped waves rushing past in a dizzying blur beneath him, and clenched his teeth. At first the metal refused to budge. He cursed it and tried again. This time he was sure he felt it give a little. He eased off, caught his breath, reached down and tried again. *Yes!* It was definitely moving.

Then the edge of the twisted piece of

metal snapped off and went flying, and because he wasn't expecting it he rolled backward with it and would have rolled right off the leading edge of the wing if Kimani hadn't quickly pulled in the slack and held him firm.

Gus slowly worked his way back to the damaged flap. The plane dipped beneath him, then leveled off again. Now that the outer edge had snapped off, a shorter, blunter piece of metal was all that remained stuck in the mechanism.

Again he tried to bend the piece of metal. Again it refused to move. He tore the spare screwdriver out of the wing and tried using it as a lever.

It worked.

Slowly the piece of metal started straightening out. He stopped for a moment, looked back over one shoulder and offered a hurried thumbs-up. Then he gave the shard a final pull and it was free.

Renee's voice came over the intercom. 'What's happening back there?'

Kimani looked in the direction of the cockpit and shouted: 'Try it now!' She didn't hear him, so Mark, who was closer, repeated the order with all the strength he could muster, though it cost him and he blacked out temporarily.

Out on the wing Gus heard an ominous grating sound. He tensed, fully prepared for this not to work. But then the flaps tilted and relief washed over him. He looked back at Kimani and gestured that the statesman should start drawing him back in. His face split by a huge grin, Kimani started doing just that.

It was then that Cotton slammed the butt of his gun down on the Secretary-General's head.

16

Cotton, feeling more dead than alive, looked down at the unconscious man and the makeshift seatbelt-rope running out through his loose fingers, then out through the ragged hole in the fuselage. He saw Gus at the same moment that Gus, alerted by the sudden slackening of the lifeline, saw him.

Cotton raised the gun and fired.

The bullets ripped holes in the wing directly in front of Gus. Instinctively he flinched, let go on the left-hand screwdriver handle and all at once was hanging on for dear life with the right, the crude lifeline now whipping loosely around him.

In the cockpit, Renee heard the snap of gunfire and looked back through the open cockpit door to see Cotton standing over the unconscious Kimani, shooting through the hole.

'Damn!'

She did the only thing she could in the

circumstances. She quickly cranked the yoke sideways, making the already unstable aircraft rock even more violently.

In the main cabin, Cotton staggered back, away from the hole. On the wing, Gus almost lost his grip on the left-hand screwdriver, then made a lunge and grabbed the right-hand one.

Cotton regained his balance, turned and aimed the gun down the aisle toward the cockpit.

At his feet Kimani suddenly lunged for Cotton, grabbed him clumsily around the legs and threw him backward. The bullet punched a hole in the curved ceiling.

For a moment terrorist and statesman wrestled for possession of the gun. Cotton was wounded, had lost blood, was weak, but in that moment he was also pumped full of anger and adrenalin, and that mixture gave him additional strength. He pushed Kimani away from him. Kimani stumbled back and collapsed in the aisle. Cotton dragged himself up and snap-aimed at the Secretary-General —

Gus suddenly filled the hole in the fuselage, saw what was about to happen and dove at Cotton. His weight sent them both sprawling in a spill of arms and legs. Cotton swore, his grimace revealing blood-stained teeth. He tried to hit Gus alongside the head with the gun but Gus avoided the blow and belted him on the jaw.

Kimani staggered to his feet, turned, saw Renee trying to divide her attention between flying the plane and watching the fight, and there, beyond the windshield by perhaps half a mile, he spotted a tiny gray oblong vessel — the *Kitty Hawk*.

'Speedbird Five, Speedbird Five, we have you on visual. Copy.'

'Roger that, *Kitty Hawk.*'

'I'm turning you over to the Flight Controller, Speedbird Five. He'll guide you in. Good luck to you.'

Gus continued hammering at Cotton, but Cotton took it all, too fired-up to stay down. He grabbed Gus's head and tried to bite his ear off. But again Gus reared back, out of reach, and all the while the lurching SST and its escort of Tomcats skimmed along above the choppy waves. Ahead the *USS Kitty Hawk* grew larger and larger, but as far as Renee could see it was nowhere near large enough to accommodate a successful landing.

Then Gus got lucky. He hooked a fist into Cotton's stomach, doubling him over. The air rushed out of him and he went down to his knees. Gus quickly slammed his fist into the side of Cotton's head, again, again, again —

Cotton went over in a heap, lay there unmoving.

Breathing hard, Gus grasped him and threw him into a seat, buckled him up, turned to Kimani. 'Are . . . you . . . all right . . . sir?'

Kimani had taken a handkerchief from his pocket and was using it to staunch the flow of blood from the cut on his neck. 'I'll live,' he said. Then he cracked a smile. 'Of course, I can't say for how *long* . . . '

Gus returned the smile with a crooked, beaten one of his own. It hurt his swollen lips. 'Grab a seat in back and get yourself buckled, sir,' he said. 'Make as much use as you can of all these blankets and pillows.'

'In a moment. I'll help your injured man to safety first.'

'Thank you. Right now my place is up there, beside — '

' — your woman?' asked Kimani.

Gus' smile broadened. Then he staggered along the aisle until he reached the cockpit.

The radio was squawking as he fell into the co-pilot's seat. 'Speedbird Five, Speedbird Five, this is Shepherd, Landing Signals Officer, HMS *Kitty Hawk*. Do you read me, Speedbird Five?'

Renee looked at Gus, at the battered state of him, and told herself that at least he was still alive. Clearing her throat she spoke into her headset: 'Loud and clear, *Kitty Hawk*.'

'Captain Gunn says you've never landed on a flat-top.'

'Wish I could say he was wrong.'

'It's not as hard as it looks.'

'From up here that deck looks *real* hard.'

'Think of it as three football fields long. You can land on three football fields, can't you?'

'I guess we're about to find out.'

'Just do everything I tell you, Captain, and it'll be a piece of cake.'

'Okay,' Renee said calmly. 'Let's do this.'

★ ★ ★

From the deck of the carrier, the aptly-named LSO Shepherd watched the crippled, low-flying SST approaching the stern. In all his years aboard flat-tops, he'd never seen anything like this, and it was awe-inspiring. 'You're coming in too low, Speedbird Five,' he said into his headset. 'Pull up a little . . . little more . . . easy, easy . . . that's better . . . now level off . . . raise the starboard wing . . . that's it . . . you're doing fine . . . just fine . . . '

From where she was sitting, though, watching the carrier hurtling ever closer, Renee didn't think she was doing fine at all. The *Kitty Hawk* seemed to be rushing at her impossibly fast . . . the tiny figure of the LSO crouched in position ahead of her, signaling madly with his batons.

'Whatever happens, Gus, I love you,' she said without looking at him.

He glanced at her profile. 'What was that you were saying about the time and the place?'

The stern of the carrier rushed closer and closer. Renee said suddenly: 'I can't do this.'

'The hell you can't!' Gus barked.

'Steady . . . steady,' said Shepherd. 'Okay, that's real good, Speedbird, you're doing fine. Now, flaps and landing gear — *down!*'

Renee, wholly focused on flying now, pointed at a bank of switches. 'Flip all those down.'

'Got 'em,' said Gus.

He did as he was told, and lights flashed on to indicate that the landing gear was lowering into position.

Renee pointed to another bank of switches. 'Now those two.'

Wordlessly, Gus flipped them down. Lights signaled that the flaps were lowering.

'Now go back and buckle yourself in beside Mark and Kimani.'

'I'm fine right where I am,' he said.

'I'm not kidding, Gus.'

'Neither am I. I've already seen the in-flight movie. This is something I *haven't* seen before.'

'Well, let's just hope you live to tell the tale.'

The plane was less than a hundred yards away now, and suddenly every fiber of her being was concentrated on the LSO and the movements of his batons.

'Ren?' said Gus.

'Not now, Gus.'

'But I've got to know.'

'Know what?'

'When this is all over, will you marry me?'

She rolled her eyes. 'God, don't you ever give up?'

'I'll take that as a yes.'

'Not so fast. What about a baby?'

Before Gus could reply, the lip of the flight deck loomed right at them and then disappeared under the nose-cone.

Renee said: 'Ohhhhh-shitttt . . . '

The aircraft barely missed the safety nets stretched across the stern of the

251

carrier and crunch-landed on the deck. It hit with a jolt, bounced and then Renee was slamming on the brakes and reversing the jet-engine thrust.

The Concorde bounced a second time and the landing gear buckled under the stress and collapsed altogether. The plane belly-flopped along the flight deck, a rooster-tail of sparks flying up as the undercarriage ground against the steel deck.

One of the cables snagged a buckled piece of the crumpled landing gear and snapped. A second cable caught on it and held. The plane slowed a little, but it was about four times heavier than a fighter and this too snapped with a sound like gunfire.

Still Renee fought with the controls, trying to keep the aircraft from spinning entirely out of control. Gus could only watch, tight-lipped, white-knuckled.

In the main cabin, Cotton suddenly snapped back to consciousness. For a moment he had no idea where he was. Then he realized by the tilt and shudder of the plane that they were landing, or trying to.

His eyes shuttled everywhere, finally settled on his fallen Uzi, lying forgotten in the aisle a few rows ahead. Still groggy, he fumbled to unbuckle his seatbelt. When it unclasped, he fell off the seat to his knees and set about trying to reach the Uzi.

With the landing gear gone, the Concorde slid sled-like on its belly and twin, box-shaped jet engines. Its long downslanted nose-cone was still higher than the crash nets and the aircraft hurtled through the first one and continued on toward the second. It scythed through the crash net as if it wasn't even there, its momentum barely slowing.

Then came the third crash net, and Renee dared to hope that their speed had slowed enough for this one to actually arrest their forward plunge.

It didn't.

Now there was an additional complication. The plane was changing direction, angling away from the center of the flight deck toward the churning sea beyond.

The port-side engine, still grinding along the deck and leaving bright sparks in its wake, hit the net and was ripped off the wing. It crashed into the yellow equipment lining the left edge of the flight deck and the engine itself exploded, hurling flaming debris everywhere.

As the plane slewed sideways Cotton was thrown across the aisle and slammed into the seats. He slumped to the floor, dazed, tilted his head, saw the Uzi still just beyond his reach and once again stretched his right arm toward it.

The Concorde raced on across the deck, leaving great, painful-looking gouges in its wake. Fires had broken out all along the deck, and fire-crews were everywhere, fighting to smother them before they could spread.

The plane careened on, spun partway around. The tip of the starboard wing smashed into the base of the superstructure and crumpled. The force of the collision threw Captain Gunn and his staff off their feet.

Still the SST continued to slide, completely out of control now. The only thing blocking its path from the end of the carrier and the ocean beyond was the yellow crane — seventy tons of machinery hoping to halt the momentum of something thirty tons heavier.

In the cockpit Renee yelled: 'We've got to get out of here — *now!*'

Gus needed no second urging. He hit the seatbelt release at the same time she did, came up out of his seat and grabbed her by the arm, yanked her up and pushed her out of the cockpit ahead of him.

The crane came closer, closer, closer —

The flimsy nose of the Concorde wrinkled and crushed into the crane. The weight and momentum of the aircraft, though slowed considerably by the nets and cables, pushed the crane inexorably toward the end of the carrier. The crumpled nose section was then driven back through the cockpit, crushing the pilot and co-pilot's seats.

The slowed aircraft continued to slide forward, compressing the fuselage together like the folds in a paper fan. Renee and Gus sprinted along the aisle to the back of the aircraft, always only feet from the wrenching, crumpling fuselage that screeched like a banshee behind them.

They ran straight past Cotton without even seeing him.

He flung himself out from between the seats, Uzi in hand. He took aim; then became aware of the floor rucking up beneath his feet. He turned, saw the plane folding itself together in his direction and —

His scream was lost in the sound of compacting metal as it crushed and then completely engulfed him.

Gus and Renee reached Kimani and Mark. There was nowhere else to run. Gus grabbed Renee, held her close, turned and watched Cotton die.

Outside, the now-mangled crane had become part of the twisted framework of the SST. Its huge weight continued to slow the sliding plane, but it was still anyone's guess whether or not it would stop the Concorde from plunging into the sea.

Then the craft slowed and slewed a little more, and finally . . . wonder of wonders . . . it ground to a halt.

★　★　★

Gus and Renee sat together in the aisle, looking at the mass of crunched metal that had finally stopped compacting barely two feet from them. When he managed to find his voice, Gus said: 'Know what?'

Renee cleared her throat. 'Tell me.'

'Flying by Concorde is highly over-rated,' he said

She grinned and gently brushed his chin with her fist. They looked at each other for the space of several heartbeats, and then they kissed.

Halfway through they remembered they weren't alone, and pulled apart so that they could turn and check on Kimani and Mark.

From his cocoon of pillows and blankets, Mark, his pale face flushed now, croaked: 'Please . . . don't mind us.'

They didn't. They went ahead and kissed and held each other and this time there was a fervor in them that could never be extinguished.

'Hey . . . you guys okay?' called a voice from outside the wreck.

'We're just fine,' Gus replied. 'In fact, I can truthfully say we couldn't be better.'

17

After that there was only the cleaning up to do. The fires were extinguished. The damaged vehicles were cleared away. The ruined crash-nets were taken down and temporary repairs were made to the scorched and cratered flight deck.

Gus, Renee, Kimani and Mark were helped down from the wreckage, taken to the medical quarters and checked over. Mark was operated on and was expected to make a full recovery. After a thorough debriefing, Gus, Renee and the Secretary-General were allowed to shower and change into some clean clothes — in this case, green navy fatigues.

When the Medical Officer said they could receive visitors, they finally got their chance to thank Captain Gunn and LSO Shepherd for their help.

'You people okay?' asked the Captain.

'I'll tell you when I stop shaking,' said Gus.

The captain grinned. 'Join the club.' He turned his attention to Renee. 'Hell of a job, Captain.'

'Thank you.'

Shepherd could only agree. 'I've been doing this for ten years, Captain. Never seen anything like it.'

'You never will again,' Gus promised him.

'I have some thanks to offer, as well,' said Kimani softly.

'No thanks necessary, sir,' said Gus. You pulled more than your weight back there.'

Kimani studied him. 'Have you ever been to the U.N., Mr. Novacek?'

'Sir, I haven't even been to the Statue of Liberty.'

'Neither have I. We'll make a day of it.'

Renee shook her head. ' 'Haven't been to the Statue of Liberty'? But Gus — you live in New York!'

'What can I tell you? I've been busy.'

'You've *what?*'

Not bothering to answer her, he simply took her by the hand and turned to Captain Gunn. 'Excuse me, sir,' he said.

'I was wondering . . . '

'Yes?'

'Have you ever *married* anyone, Captain?'

Gunn's mouth dropped open. 'Good God, no.'

'But you *can* do it? I mean, you *are* the captain.'

'I guess so.'

'Then if you wouldn't mind doing the honors, sir, and if *you*, Mr. Secretary, would agree to stand up and be my best man . . . '

Renee tried to pull away from him, but he knew what was bothering her and said: 'Don't worry, honey. I've been thinking long and hard about a family.'

'For how long?' she countered. 'Since the plane started to go down?'

'How about a boy *and* a girl?' he asked.

She tried to give him a stern look but it was hard to suppress her smile. 'Novacek,' she said. 'One of these days . . . '

'Today's as good as any,' he said.

And she couldn't agree more.

THE END

We do hope that you have enjoyed reading this large print book.

Did you know that all of our titles are available for purchase?

We publish a wide range of high quality large print books including:
Romances, Mysteries, Classics
General Fiction
Non Fiction and Westerns

Special interest titles available in large print are:
The Little Oxford Dictionary
Music Book, Song Book
Hymn Book, Service Book

Also available from us courtesy of Oxford University Press:
Young Readers' Dictionary
(large print edition)
Young Readers' Thesaurus
(large print edition)

For further information or a free brochure, please contact us at:
Ulverscroft Large Print Books Ltd.,
The Green, Bradgate Road, Anstey,
Leicester, LE7 7FU, England.
Tel: (00 44) **0116 236 4325**
Fax: (00 44) **0116 234 0205**

Other titles in the
Linford Mystery Library:

THE CLEVERNESS OF MR. BUDD

Gerald Verner

Responding to an urgent telephone request, solicitor Larry Graham drives to the Yorkshire Moors home of a client, Benjamin Starl, who is gravely ill. However, when Starl's secretary, Margaret Lane, shows Larry to his bedroom, his client has been brutally murdered — a knife embedded in his blood-drenched body! And soon, even more shockingly, Superintendent Budd from Scotland Yard arrives and asks if they can explain why the dead body of a strangled man is lying on the steps outside . . .

THE VANISHING DEATH

Nigel Vane

Thieves, breaking into a mortuary to steal the body of a woman, are disturbed by a police constable, and they escape, dropping their burden in the street. Then, days later, a lorry grazes a speeding car, dislodging a hamper attached to its roof. Neither vehicle stops. Inside the hamper, the police find the body of a recently murdered man whose corpse had been stolen whilst awaiting police examination. Who's behind the would-be body-snatcher — and what is their sinister purpose . . . ?

FIRESTREAK

Mike Linaker

In the twenty-first-century marshal
Thomas Jefferson Cade and his
cyborg partner, Janek, uphold the law
in the violent cities, mutant-ridden
Chemlands and lawless Outlands.
They are assigned to nail Loren Brak,
a renegade drug dealer heading west
to start his own empire. With his
shock troops, they face a formidable
enemy. Surrounded on all sides by
hostile forces, the Justice marshals
follow the bloody trail to Los Angeles
— and enter the killzone . . . guns
loaded, targets in sight.

THE SEVEN LAMPS

Gerald Verner

Jill Hartley has to take important papers to 18 Hayford Avenue, Berrydale, the home of her firm's client, Professor Locksley. But when she arrives at the neglected house she finds the front door open — the inside of the house, dark, damp and decaying. And huddled at the foot of the stairs lies a dead man, in a pool of blood, his head battered to a pulp. At Berryfield Police Station Superintendent Budd investigates this horrifying and mysterious case.

TO DREAM AGAIN

E. C. Tubb

Ralph Mancini, an officer in the United Nations Law Enforcement Agency, is dedicated to the world-wide War on Drugs. A new drug is developed, giving a uniquely effective 'trip', whereby people become God-like beings and they experience 'heaven'. The next trip is their only priority — whatever the cost. Ralph and Inspector Frere follow a tangled trail of murder, seeking the source of the peril — but will they be too late to stop it spreading across the world?